Through the fires of hell, men of steel are forged.

LEGENDS OF THE ROADS
BORN TO BE WILD
IRON CITY
NIGHTS
SUPERIOR PERFORMANCE
LEGENDARY RIDERS

IGNITE
ML NYSTROM

I0718617

SHE'S A HACKE
WITH A CAUS
H AN OUTLA
ITH A PAS
WHEN THE
LDS COLLID
THE FALLOU
COULD BUR
THEM BOT
IRON CITY
KNIGHTS

IGNITE

ML NYSTROM

HOT TREE PUBLISHING

For information, contact the publisher, Hot Tree Publishing.

WWW.HOTTREEPUBLISHING.COM

EDITING: HOT TREE EDITING

COVER DESIGNER: BOOKSMITH DESIGN

E-BOOK ISBN: 978-1-923252-40-0

PAPERBACK ISBN: 978-1-923252-41-7

IGNITE

IRON CITY KNIGHTS
BOOK 1

ML NYSTROM

HOT TREE PUBLISHING

To Katie Roberts,

May your cute smile always shine big, bright, and beautiful.

1

"No, ma'am, that is not right! I put too much money in the refund. I'm so sorry, ma'am. I will need you to do something for me or else I will lose my job."

Jazz tried not to laugh at the pretend panic in the heavily accented voice on the other end of the line. She adjusted her headset before setting her hands back on the keyboard and typing rapidly while she spoke into the voice modulator. Her bright young soprano came out as a rough old alto. "Oh my, I'm so very sorry, dearie. What can I do to make it right?"

File after file appeared on a long list on her screen. The grin on her face grew with delight, and she deleted them all with a satisfying tap of her finger on the mouse.

"I need you to go to your car and go to Target and get three gift cards in the amount of five hundred dollars each."

Jazz rolled her eyes and pressed her lips together to stifle her amusement. "Oh my goodness gracious, I don't have a car."

"You don't have a car?"

"No, my grandson borrowed it last week and hasn't come to see me since. I think maybe he stole it. Can you imagine someone stealing from an old person like me?" It got harder to keep her laughter in check. She hacked into another page on the caller's computer. Jackpot! Row by row, she deleted all the banking information she found.

"Can you borrow your neighbor's car?"

You're determined to get those gift cards, aren't you? "I don't have any neighbors. They all moved away when the industry dried up. No jobs, you see."

"Please, ma'am, do you have any way to get to the Target?"

She kept typing. "I could use my power chair, but it'll take a long time. I'm not sure my battery will last all the way there and back. It's a long trip from my little house out in the boonies. I'll have to recharge at the store."

"Please, ma'am, I need to get this money back. Can you do a wire transfer?"

Jazz had finished with the banking files and made one last hacking foray. She found the guy's phishing program and, with absolute relish, deleted that one in its entirety. Finally, she uploaded one of several custom-designed viruses to the scammer's computer and let it loose.

"Look at your files, Sparky." Jazz dropped the fake voice.

"What is happening?" Confusion tinged the man's words.

"You're S-O-L, asshole. How dare you try to scam old people out of their hard-earned money. Lowlifes like you should be in prison."

"Motherfu—"

Jazz didn't wait to hear the man's curses. She hung up and leaned back in her padded desk chair. Freya jumped onto her lap and started purring. The black-and-white cat had shown up one afternoon and moved in as if she owned the small house.

"Perfect start to a perfect day, eh?" Jazz stroked the feline's arching back and listened to the contented rumble.

A text message popped up on her screen, and she glanced at it.

Bomber123: I got four last night. What did you get?

Jazz leaned forward and typed one-handed.

Jazzyhands: Only two, but I screwed one up big-time a few minutes ago. Deleted their whole friggin' program.

Bomber123: No shit? Bet that's going to set them back awhile.

Jazzyhands: That's the point, right?

Bomber123: Fuck yeah. You know that call center we got a few weeks ago is still out of commission?

Jazzyhands: That's good to hear. It took four of us, but tags worked well in taking those down. I think we should team up more often and go for the bigger fish. It'll save a lot more than these little ones.

Bomber123: I think your right.

Jazzyhands: You're

Bomber123: :-p~ Pbbbbbbt!

Jazzyhands: Wuv U 2. Anyhoo, I gotta go. The working class needs their morning cuppa cuppa.

Bomber123: Fine. Go be a part of capitalistic society.

Jazz didn't reply, just shut down the computer and stood up from her desk. She tapped the Starship Enterprise hanging from the ceiling with her finger before stretching her arms high overhead. Her spine popped and cracked as the bones aligned themselves. Freya meowed in protest at being dislodged from her happy perch.

"Sorry, baby. I gotta go make the donuts, as they say," Jazz informed the cat as she sauntered into the bathroom in her sleep tank and panties.

The old house was built in the early 1900s and not much more than livable when Jazz found it and fell in love. The biggest reason she wanted this house showed in the greenway just outside the front that faced the Allegheny River. She got to view the slow-moving water every morning when she woke up and peered out her bedroom window. The old plumbing had been updated sometime during the 1970s based on the gold-colored tub and tiles in the bathroom. As long as the water was hot, Jazz didn't care about the outdated look. She had bigger issues to handle. Some paint, area rugs over the worn linoleum, and lots of her favorite sci-fi knickknacks scattered around fit her decor theme. Nothing else was needed.

The shower streamed over her black-and-blue hair. She did the bright ombre as a dare in college and liked the contrast against her dark roots enough to keep it. Ten years later, her parents still gave her disapproving looks when she made time to visit. Her younger sister flat-out hated it.

"You're almost thirty years old, Jasmine. Don'cha think it's time for you to get serious about your life?" Liz had criticized on more than one occasion.

Yeah, like *she* got serious about *hers*? Three kids by two men and one pending divorce had Jazz's younger sister moving back in with their parents, and she showed no signs of making any progress on her own. Her sour attitude toward anything and every-thing gave Jazz all the more reason to keep the different color.

The youngest sibling, her brother, Hugo, loved her hair and made a point of telling everyone as much at the forced family gatherings. The next one would be on Easter Sunday in a few weeks. Jazz dreaded it already and was trying to figure a way out. No doubt Hugo was doing the same.

She ran a hand through the thick locks. "I should

totally do a touch-up. Do I dare add some purple or pink?"

Freya jumped up and sat in the sink on the small vanity, since there was no room anywhere else for her. Jazz towel-dried her waves and ran a comb through the wet strands. "Don't judge. You get free room and board, yeah?"

Fifteen minutes later, she finished dressing and was set to go. "Love you, Frey-Frey."

The cat meowed in protest.

"Shit, I forgot. Hold on."

Jazz ripped open a cat food pouch and dumped it into a small bowl. "Later, tater."

The house sat in a dip, and the back faced the narrow street with a short bridge from the road to a second-floor entrance. There was no yard to mow, just the occasional trimming of the brush that grew right up to the outer walls of her house. The only place for her to park her car was a recess spot off the street some yards away. Living alone in this tiny Pittsburgh suburb had never bothered her. Since she didn't have to cross any of the river bridges, most of the time, she simply biked the half mile to work.

The sun peeked over the horizon, sending pale rays of color across the black sky. Frequent insomnia made early mornings her thing throughout her twenties. She loved being awake before the sun to watch it rise as she started a new day. It wasn't odd for her to take catnaps during the day or just after dinner so she'd be up when most people were still dreaming.

She pedaled down the empty streets, pausing only to tuck the scarf over her mouth and nose. The cold, crisp air blew against her face. It was that time of year between winter and spring where it was anyone's guess what the weather would be. By the afternoon, the sun might raise the temperature to summer levels. She hoped the chilly mornings were on their way out as she coasted across Baker Ave and into the back lot of the coffee and cake shop.

This older neighborhood held no appeal for the tourists. A scattered mix of tightly placed row houses and industrial businesses dotted the long stretches that gave off a "keep driving" vibe. It also helped that a big steel plant stood just a few miles down the road. Workers often came in between shifts to grab coffees and cakes or just sit for a little while in a place with cleaner air to breathe.

Bill and Madge Comer owned the bakery and coffee shop, simply named Coffee and Cakes. Madge was already in the building, mixing ingredients in a large bowl. "Grab those sheets, eh?" she said when Jazz entered.

The yeasty smell hit Jazz's nose as she brought the long baking pans of risen flat dough to Madge's workstation. Moravian sugar cakes were a specialty of hers, and some people drove miles out of their way to pick up the traditional European treat.

A tray of twisted square soft pretzels lay on the table ready to go in the display case next to an assortment of miniature shoofly pies, whoopie pies, bagels, and other Pittsburgh treats.

Jazz grabbed a plain apron. "You stay up all night again?"

Madge shrugged. "Someone's got to get the work done." The large woman's face had long bags under the eyes and a worn-down demeanor. She started jabbing her fingers into the flattened dough to make the surface bumpy with lots of divots.

"Do you ever sleep?"

Another shrug from Madge as she carefully poured the butter, cinnamon, and brown sugar mixture over the raw cake, watching it fill the holes. "I'll sleep when I'm dead."

Jazz wanted to hug the woman but knew better. She lifted the heavy baking sheets and slid them into the oven. Madge would stay there until the morning rush died down, then walk two streets over to the row house she and Bill owned. She'd cook the local favorite of dippy eggs and scrapple for Bill, then help him get dressed and wheel him over to sit in the bakery for the afternoon. The man's lungs were shot from breathing toxic air while working in the steel mill for over forty years, and now the coffee shop was the only income they had outside the pitiful settlement pension and meager social security. At one time, they had a nice-sized savings account, but that was stolen from them.

It was one of the major reasons Jazz had joined up with the online group of scammer hunters and shielders.

Madge shuffled her bulk to the front counter. "Just about time."

She slid open the top and bottom door locks just as the first wave of factory people started in. "Morning, boys. Come on in."

For the next hour, Jazz made coffee to keep the self-service carafe full and worked the espresso machine for fancier drinks. Madge served pastries, rang up purchases at the register, and chatted with the men. Some were on their way home, and some were headed to the mill for the day shift. The coffee shop had become a neighborhood staple, and a big part of their business happened during these morning hours.

Jazz glanced up at the clock. Almost seven. Her heart fluttered a bit. It was about time for—

The bell rang over the door, and her breath caught as a thrill buzzed through her stomach.

Wolf stood in the doorway, all six feet of him. It was all Jazz could do not to sigh at the hunk of sexy gorgeousness she looked forward to seeing every day. So many men sported long bushy beards now, but he kept his trimmed short and close. The style accentuated his high cheekbones and square jaw. His dark brown waves were tied back at the nape of his neck and perfectly showed off the narrow gray streak that flowed from the top left side of his forehead. Jazz wanted to ask him about it, but the words never formed when his green eyes landed on her. Green was the closest color description she had. Sometimes they looked blue, sometimes gold, but always with a greenish hue.

She could stare at his eyes for hours.

Wolf came in every morning, and from what she'd figured out, he usually came directly from his job. He didn't work at the steel mill, but his cut showed his membership in a local motorcycle club, the Iron City Knights. They had some sort of machine shop down the street right next to the strip club they owned. Jazz had never been inside either place. Reason one? The only bike she owned operated by two pedals and a chain. Reason two? She was not a stripper, and her body didn't have the assets to be one.

The neighborhood was rough by some standards, but the coffee shop, the Comers' house, and surrounding businesses had the protection of the biker gang.

Correction: biker *club*.

Jazz set up the espresso machine for double shots as she heard the velvety tones of Wolf's voice. "Morning, Madge. Bill up yet?"

"Nah. Too early. I gotta go get him in about an hour. It's too slippy for him right now."

The hiss of the steamer drowned out anything else Madge and Wolf said. Jazz took a breath as she made the latte in a paper go-cup. Wolf never stayed unless Bill was there. Then the two men would sit at one of the square tables, sometimes getting into a chess game and conversing. On Bill's bad days, Wolf would simply sit in silent company with the old man.

He never paid any attention to Jazz other than a random "Thanks" when she handed him his morning cup of joe. In fact, he seldom noticed her at all. She bit her lip as she wiped off the stainless-steel nozzle. *I bet he doesn't even know my name.*

She finished the latte and popped a lid on top before handing it to him. His fingers brushed hers as he accepted it, and the contact sent another jolting zap through her body, already mega-aware of his presence.

Gah, Jazz, quit doing the schoolgirl thing. You're a friggin' grown-ass woman. Act like it!

She managed to smile at his disembodied "Thanks" and moved back to the machine to start the next order.

"Hey."

It was a single word, but it came out as an attention-grabbing command. Her heart flipped over and started doing burpees in her chest. She swallowed the sudden rush of saliva in her mouth and turned with a bright smile. *Don't show him you're nervous, don't show him you're nervous, don't show him you're...* "Yes?"

"Wrap up a couple Danishes for me, yeah? Raspberry."

Her brain short-circuited. *Sure thing. No problem. "No thing." Holy frig!* "I mean, sure problem."

She felt her face flame as she bent low behind the counter to hide while she wrapped two of the biggest pastries in waxed paper.

"Bill's callin' me to get 'im now." Madge slid her

cell phone closed. "Can't stand not to be in the middle of things. Mind helpin' me?"

Wolf grabbed the paper bag Jazz set on the glass display case without looking in her direction. "I'll walk over with you."

Jazz breathed easier after they left. She made herself a latte in one of the big white china mugs and swirled an elaborate leaf pattern in the top. Wolf's effect on her dissipated, and her self-castigation started.

Why do you have to be such a dummy dork around him? Stop this moony crap and be an adult.

Ugh. Perhaps someday she'd get over her crush on the man and move on.

2

Wolf swallowed the last of his coffee. It was still good, even though it had gone cold. He tossed the cup at the dumpster as he entered the back of the building that housed the MC's strip club and hangout. It bounced off the edge, and he swore as he turned to go back and pick it up. Madge's blue-coiffed helper knew her way around the spitting espresso machine. Cute kid. She looked like she'd just graduated from high school, even though he knew she was older. Late twenties, maybe? Nice hair.

The shy girl disappeared from his thoughts as he joined the group of men sitting around one of the bar tables. Scrap and Baghouse were senior members of the club with Melter right behind. Camshaft and

Crossman were the youngest. Wolf and Quillon sat in the middle. The only one missing was Go-Kart. "We having church or something?"

Scrap shook his head and raised a scarred three-fingered hand to the black patch over his missing eye. "Nah. Just talkin' about some stuff. Nothin' formal."

Scrap was the president, owner of the strip club, and the oldest of the group. He'd been a steelworker for years until an accident with a rolling mill nearly took him out. The company had ignored safety precautions for years until Scrap got caught in the machine. His body had a myriad of scars from the incident, and it was a miracle he only lost his eye and part of his hand. The upside? The company didn't want a big scandalous and expensive lawsuit, so they'd settled on a very generous compensation with Scrap, one that allowed him to purchase and start the machine shop and the titty bar. Melter called it Attic, and the name stuck. Later, Quillon bought out the machine shop but still employed a number of club members.

"Camshaft said the Slaggers were riding through our area last night." Baghouse shook his head. "Stupid name for a bunch of jagoffs."

"Those jagoffs are growing. I understand they've

taken over the Lincoln Park area across the river and are looking to expand on our side." Melter sprinkled some dried pot onto a rolling paper and licked the edge. "They're drug dealers, n'at."

Wolf gave an incredulous huff. "You're rolling a blunt and calling them drug dealers?"

Melter held up the white stick. "This ain't drugs. It's only weed. Those guys do the big stuff like pills n'at meth shit."

Wolf didn't argue with the older man. Melter was also a veteran of the steel mill and had the scars to prove it. "I doubt they're interested in our side of the river. They got enough business to keep them happy on the southside."

The older man grunted, showing his waning interest in the rival club. "Didjoo bring any Danishes from Bill and Madge's place?"

Wolf smiled as he handed over the white bag. "I have one left. Figured you'd claim it."

Baghouse didn't want to let the subject drop. "So, what are we gonna do about them?"

The bag crinkled as Melter pulled out the wax-paper-covered treat. "'Bout who?"

Baghouse threw his hands in the air. "Christ on a cracker, the Slaggers!"

"Nothing." Scrap snatched the Danish and took a big bite. White icing smeared around his wiry gray beard.

"Motherfucker!" Melter yelled and grabbed it back.

"Yinz fuck around too much," Baghouse grumbled. "That hippie guy up at the vape shop said those fuckers came by last week, asking about business n'at. He said they wanted him to store some shit for them. Kinda like a distribution center. Said they wouldn't take no for an answer."

Wolf shrugged. A night of running security at the titty bar made him bone-tired and ready to go home and crash. However, he was also the club's unofficial mediator and enforcer. He flipped around a high-backed chair and sat, leaning his elbows on the top. "The hippie guy agree to it?"

"He said no, but it's only a matter of time. Rumor has it the Slaggers got some big-time connections comin' from New York City. International pipeline straight to here."

"Why the hell would a big international drug cartel be interested in a small-time vape shop?" Melter said around a mouthful of pastry. "That shit only happens in movies."

"Not the big-time guys who make the shit. It's the

guys who bring in the goods who're looking for new places to distribute and sell."

Wolf's eyes grew grittier by the minute. "Then we have nothing to worry about, right? If they have their spot staked out, that's got nothing to do with us."

Baghouse made a sound of disgust. "It's not right."

"Maybe not, but as long as they stay out of our business, we'll stay out of theirs."

"Yeah, sure. We'll see how long that lasts. Yinz know damn well if those fuckers move anywhere near here, there's gonna be trouble. We've never had a turf war with anyone, and we don't want to start now. We need to keep our eyes on this before it becomes a real problem."

Wolf sighed as he stood. "I'm not concerned about anything right now except getting some sleep. Crossman, you're on tonight, yeah?"

The younger man nodded.

"Cool. I'm outta here."

Wolf left the club and mounted his big blue Honda. Harleys were great for cruising on long stretches of road, but in the city, Hondas and Kawasakis did better because they had water-cooled engines instead of air-cooled. A blaze of colorful orange flames streaked down the front and side fairings from the custom paint job he got at a rally down in North Carolina. Dodge, a member of the Dragon Runners MC, did it for him. The man was definitely an artist.

The ride to his place wasn't very long, but he did have to drive by the steel plant. Acrid fumes drifted from the place where iron was heated, purified, blended, and formed into steel. Wolf's father had lived, worked, and died in that plant, his lungs shot from breathing the toxic air for so many years before OSHA came in and forced it to code. Bill was the only one left from that crew, and Wolf had a soft spot for the man. Madge worked hard to keep the bakery going and take care of her husband, and it bordered on more than she could handle. What other choice did she have, though? Money had to be made, and bills had to be paid.

Wolf's thoughts drifted to the young woman who'd assisted them for several years now. Madge probably didn't pay a lot, and he was sure there were no benefits other than free pastries. She must live on a shoestring budget or had another job. Perhaps she had a sugar daddy packed away somewhere? She was pretty enough to attract one, but nah, any woman with a big income wouldn't be dressing in thrift-store glam or working in a bakery, right?

"Jazz," Madge had called her a few times, though it was usually "Jazzy," and more than once she'd mentioned how much she and Bill depended on the young woman. Wolf had seen her there and noticed her pretty blushes every time she had to serve him. Yeah, he got a kick out of that, and he made a point of messing with her to see her cheeks go pink and hear her screw up her words.

He pulled up to a house in an older neighborhood. Like many in this area, the long and thin structure had very little yard in front and no space between it and the house on the left side. The right side butted up to an overgrown tangle of trees that threatened to engulf the house one day. Behind it, some yards away, sat a set of abandoned train tracks.

Delia Best, his eighty-nine-year-old neighbor and landlady, lived in the bottom half, and he occupied the top. The almost-nonagenarian rarely left her home, as she no longer drove and relied on her church people or Wolf to take her places. She had a son and a daughter, but one lived in Florida and the other in California. She spent much of her time watching TV or YouTube cat videos and scrolling through Facebook. It bothered Wolf that Delia was essentially by herself, and he did as much for her as he could to help her out.

"Wolf, is that you?" Delia's wavering voice came from the open door, and the thin, frail woman appeared, bent over an old-fashioned metal walker with small wheels on the front and yellow tennis balls on the back legs. Life hadn't been easy for her, but so far, she'd avoided any major falls or health issues. She waved a square paper on a stick at her face, making her wispy hair fluff. Delia's part of the house had fans but no air-conditioning. He had a window unit upstairs if the summer heat became too much. The shade was one advantage of the encroaching greenery.

"Yeah. You need something, Dee?" She told him once that she loved it when he called her Dee. It made her feel special and wanted. "No, thank you. Robin and Barry from the church are coming by later to take me to the grocery store. I saw in the paper that bratwursts are on sale. If I get some, will you join me for dinner?"

"You bet. I'm gonna go crash for a few hours. I'll get up and do *Jeopardy!* with you later, yeah?"

Her faded blue eyes lit up. "That would be lovely."

He hugged the fragile woman gently. She charged a ridiculously low rent, but he added an extra hundred every month as she cooked several nights a week for him. Sometimes, he was the only person she saw in a day's time.

"Call upstairs if you need anything."

"Enjoy your nap."

The top of the house was composed of two large rooms with a bathroom in between. Wolf used one as a bedroom and the other as a kind of den. He owned very little furniture, just the basic bed-dresser-night-stand setup. He did have a couch in the other room, but most of the time, he used his recliner to watch the big flat-screen he had mounted on the wall. A small dorm-sized refrigerator sat in one corner of his den, filled with his favorite Iron City brews and bottled waters. A set of plastic white shelves held snacks and a microwave, but that was as much kitchen as he wanted or needed.

Wolf considered ordering food, but sleep called to him more. Instead, he opened his fridge to grab a water bottle and chugged down half of it in one go. The night had been a typical one. The dancers danced. The men drank and stared. Money flowed. Nothing out of the ordinary. Nothing special or significant.

Sometimes boring was nice. He'd take it any day over his past job.

He took the three steps needed to get to his

bedroom, where he promptly stripped down to his boxers and fell onto his back. The cheap metal frame squeaked and bounced under his weight. Wolf heaved a great sigh and closed his eyes. Nope, nothing out of the ordinary. No drama. No glitches. No problems.

So why did he have this uneasy feeling in his gut?

3

"No, no, no, no! You don't press the Windows key for that!"

The irritated voice blared through Jazz's headset, and she bit her lip to keep from laughing. "I'm sorry. I thought you said press it. My bad."

Tonight, instead of a confused old woman, she'd opted for a ditzy, clueless girly-girl. Appropriate for her mood, as she'd spent several days chastising herself about her brief weird interaction with Wolf. *"No thing." "Sure problem." He must think I'm an absolute nutjob!*

The last few mornings, he'd come in, grabbed his coffee, and gabbed with Bill. He didn't speak to her, but he did give her a finger twitch and one of those head things where his chin jerked upward in a "what's up" gesture. Nothing else.

Argh! I'm such a dweeby dorky dork! Enough. Focus on the task at hand, yeah? "Are you talking about the key with the squares on it? Oh, I got it now!"

She scrolled farther down, then highlighted and deleted a big set of files that included several programs. In the background, she heard other agents and guessed she was dealing with another call center.

"We have to start over, ma'am. Don't touch anything this time."

Oh no, you don't, buddy. She watched as the scammer tried to take over her home screen, and then she blocked him again.

He cursed in Hindi, and she had to mute herself before the mirth she held back exploded. A glance at her Death Star clock told her she'd been on the phone with this guy for over two hours. She had a bet going with Bomber123 about how long they could keep a call going. Bomber had the record at three hours and twenty-three minutes. During that time, he managed to keep three scammers going until he hacked their systems and deleted their files. Jazz had heard of other shielders who'd done single calls for as much as eight hours. She wasn't sure she had the stamina for that, but she admitted to having fun when stringing along a scammer for a long time.

Another outburst came from the scammer. "You have to stop pressing the key!"

Jazz took a breath to tell the guy off and that she'd already caught on to his act, but her fingers slipped and she hit some keys in a random sequence on her computer. The screen blipped once and then filled with scrolling pages.

"Holy shit!" she said out loud, forgetting to use the voice modulator.

Dates, times, names, and numbers—thousands of them—appeared from all over the world, showing active calls and amounts being collected, all in real time. This was a view of the call center's entire operation. Millions upon millions in different currencies were being added, converted to dollars, and then moved from place to place to clean it. Deposits, withdrawals, new accounts created, old ones deleted, and more popping up as she watched. She had no idea how she'd hacked into this live feed, but it was both amazing and terrifying as hell. How many people did it take to support this kind of volume?

And what kind of havoc did it wreak on the hundreds of people getting robbed as the numbers flowed?

"What was that, ma'am?"

This was huge. She wished she had time to contact Bomber or Copperpot or any other shielder, but no one else showed online. If she tried to get further into this ginormous network, she could insert her special virus and shut down the whole operation. At least in theory. If not, she would at least do enough damage to slow it down.

Jazz remembered the guy was on the line waiting for an answer. She resumed her character and started typing again. "Oh, nothing. My... uh... roommate is playing video games in the other room, and she cusses, like, all the time. Isn't that awful?"

She kept going, not giving the scammer any time to speak as she worked. She spun a tale of her BFF marrying a no-good man who up and left her when she had cancer, how expensive the cancer treatments were, the bad attitude of her other friends and parents, anything her brain drummed up to keep the guy occupied while her fingers danced over the keyboard. She just needed to find a way in.

Her screen pinged with a notice, and she saw a call being made to a familiar area code. Someone from this center had contacted someone right here in Pittsburgh. A woman named Delia Best. Jazz jumped on it immediately. The Wi-Fi at this person's house was slow as fuck, but she hoped they had call-waiting.

"Hey, my mom is calling me. Be right back."

"No, don—"

She switched off to dial the local number. Her earpiece rang several times before someone picked up.

"Hello?" From the accent and tone, it sounded like an elderly woman. A scammer's perfect target, and Jazz's opportunity to piggyback from a different source into the massive network.

"Ma'am, did someone just call you saying they're from Amazon?"

"Yes," the wavering voice answered. "How did you know? Who is this?"

"I'm Jazzyhands, and the call you just got before mine is a scam. Are they still on the line?"

"A scam? I've heard of those. Yes, he's on the other line. A very nice young man."

Cool beans! Jazz's fingers scrolled and typed in a flurry of motions to trace back and link into the scammer's computer. "You need to hang up, and if they call you back, ignore it."

"But he says they have a refund for me."

"Have you bought anything recently from Amazon?"

"Well... no. It's been a few months since I ordered anything."

"I'm sorry to tell you this, ma'am, but there's no refund. These people will do their best to take as much of your money as they can."

"How do I know *you're* not the scammer?"

Good question, Jazz thought. Anonymity was essential for the shielder to be effective, but she didn't have time to spin anything else but the truth. "Because I'm right here in Pittsburgh, just off the river in the Morningside neighborhood near the zoo. I work for Madge and Bill Comer at their coffee shop down on Miller. You know it? Coffee and Cakes? They got scammed out of their life savings a few years ago. Did you hear about it?"

"Oh, I love the zoo. I used to take my children there. I know Madge from another church. She makes the best sugar cakes."

Jazz smiled as her hands kept moving. "For sure. I love the drizzle she puts on top before baking."

"Oh, yes, that's the best way to make that kind of cake. Shame what happened to them. Are you the pretty blue-haired girl they talk about?"

Jazz nodded, even though Delia couldn't see. "Yes, I am. My name is Jasmine, but most people call me Jazz or Jazzy, or Jazzyhands online. The zoo is one of my favorite places too. Anyway, that other guy, you really need to just hang up on him. Or I'll tell you what, let me hack into the call and I'll take care of him for you, okay?"

"Do I have to pay you?"

She caught herself this time as she shook her head. "No, ma'am. This is something I do for free just to help people like you and Madge."

The silence on the end of the phone told Jazz the woman was thinking about it.

"Okay, go ahead. You need my number?"

"No, I got it covered. You just let me take over, and I'll handle these jerks. You can stay on the line if you want to hear what happens, but please don't make any noise or anything to give it away, okay?"

Hacking into a landline was difficult but not impossible. The challenge was keeping up with the scammer trying to get into her system and at the same time engaging with Delia's caller. If her computer could protest the amount of data she made it process all at once, it would have given her the finger and crashed.

It took some skilled finagling, but somehow she got it all done as she bounced from line to line. Delia's cyberattacker sounded like one of the really big call centers with pretend phone agents and pretend supervisors. The classic script of the overpaid refund started. Jazz's voice modulator didn't match the old woman's voice exactly, but the amount of money they wanted to take kept their focus locked on the scam. She found the window she needed to get into their system and pulled out the virus file.

"Take that, assholes," she muttered as she hit Send. It would take a while for the virus to work its way through the system, but it was the strongest she'd ever created and would render that network completely dead with no chance of recovery if it wasn't checked. Its potency rivaled anything else she'd ever seen, and she didn't use it every time she took down a scammer.

She watched the computer screen with glee and flailed her hands in the air, wiggling her fingers. "Gotcha!"

One by one, the live calls dropped as the scammers frantically tried to save their system. Jazz imagined a lot of curses filling the air in that place as all the transactions got blocked and their data disappeared line by line, page by page.

"Jazzyhands?" Delia's voice tentatively asked.

"I'm still here. The scammers are gone. I messed up their system pretty badly. They shouldn't bother you again."

"I'm so grateful. Thanks for helping me."

Jazz leaned back and smiled in satisfaction, and Freya jumped up onto her lap. "No problem. You have a great night. If you ever get over to the bakery, I'll treat you to a sugar cake and coffee."

4

Nassar stared at his screen as it went blank, and then the entire call center floor erupted into chaos. The floor supervisor took off his headset and threw it to the floor. Other workers jumped up from their rows of computers and cursed in panic as screen after screen shut down. In a matter of minutes, the network and its data disappeared.

All of it.

Every. Last. Byte.

Cold sweat broke out on his forehead as he punched uselessly at the keyboard. Gone. It was all gone. Not even the operating system remained. Fifty computers sat in regimented rows at this facility, and none of them would ever work again.

What the fuck just happened?

Virus. It had to be a virus, sophisticated enough to take out an entire network. Had someone targeted them? Who? Did it get all the centers on the network or just this one?

Nassar pulled out his phone. It took him three tries to scroll to the right number, as his hands were shaking so much. "Halil. What is going on? Are you still operational?"

The man's angry yell had a tinge of fear to it. "Fuck no! Nothing is working. We just reached four million for the day, and then it disappeared! The system, the money, all of it! I can't even get the computers to start up again! Useless trash!"

Nassar heard the crash of a monitor hitting the ground. If Halil's center was also down, he expected the others were too.

This was bad. Very bad. The company owned many such centers, and most of them were legitimate businesses; however, those places were used to hide and filter the millions collected by locations such as this one. Smaller centers and even individual scammers were peanuts compared to this massive money machine that skimmed from the world's population every day.

If this virus destroyed the network for this branch of the company, what did it do for the others?

Nassar hung up on Halil and quickly pressed the numbers for Samir, who worked in a center that fielded calls for a major airline. The man answered before being greeted properly.

"Oh my God, Nassar! What is happening? The network is down, and I can't get it back up. Our IT department says they can't find anything. It's just dead. How is this possible?"

"I don't know." Nassar's heart plummeted to his feet. He had no other words or suggestions. His biggest nightmare had come true.

Samir continued ranting. "We have to get this fixed!"

"I don't think we can."

Nassar hung up and placed his hands over his face. Ten years ago, he'd been a struggling tech manager with shit pay and no prospects. His wife had just given birth to their fourth child, who turned out to be another daughter, this one with special needs. This strained his budget even further and pushed his family to the brink. The company approached him with an offer of money he couldn't refuse, and for the last decade, he'd been able to afford a nice house in a high-end neighborhood and good schools. Some would call him rich, and yes, he could have spent more on a lavish lifestyle, with expensive cars and vacations, but his natural caution had him thinking ahead constantly, planning and praying the scenarios he plotted in his head would never come to pass.

Time had run out.

If this disaster was as big as he imagined, someone was going to die.

Ugly.

Violently.

Bloody.

Nassar got up from his station, keeping his eyes down. His colleagues were so busy yelling and gesturing at the dead screens that they didn't notice when he left the office and walked calmly into the locker room. He spun the combination to his locker and glanced furtively around to make sure no one else had entered behind him. The red light on the security camera didn't blink, and he was sure the network crash disabled it, yet tingles of fear traveled up and down his spine. He pushed against the back panel of the metal box and carefully slid it to the side. He'd discovered this hiding place by accident—a missing piece of cinder block left an open spot just big enough for his purposes. His fingers closed around a leather pouch and a burner phone. He opened the pouch to check the two flash drives inside. Ancient storage devices by today's standards, but they kept their data secure and untouched by the internet. One of them held his escape plan, the other insurance to see that plan through.

He tied the flat pouch around his waist and tucked it into the spot just below his belly button where his stomach hung over to hide the small bulge. His loose pants should be enough to disguise any tell-tale sign, and most men wouldn't dare to look at his crotch. Still, he felt the weight hanging there as a beacon for all to see, like he'd strapped on a target. He took several deep breaths before using the burner phone to call his wife.

"Hello?"

"Fatima, my love."

"Nassar. Is something wrong? What number is this?"

"Listen and don't argue. It's time."

"Time? What are you talking about?"

Nassar gritted his teeth in frustration. "Fatima."

She stayed silent, but he heard the slight intake of breath as she understood. "No. Please, no."

"You know what to do."

Her exhale sounded as if she'd resolved her thoughts about the coming life changes. "Yes."

"Go now. I'll meet you soon."

Last act, he thought as he took the SIM card from

his main phone with shaking fingers. He snapped it in half before stomping on the screen.

The center was still in pandemonium when he exited the building, walked down to the corner, and disappeared.

5

The bell rang over the door for the eleventy-thousandth time that morning. Jazz pulled a tray of sugar cakes from the oven and burned her fingers in the process.

"Be right there!" she yelled.

The morning rush seemed heavier, probably because she was working by herself. Bill had called Madge away with problems when he switched his oxygen tanks. That left Jazz to make coffee, take orders, run the register, and get the pastries out of the ovens before anything burned.

"Take your time."

The velvety voice sent sparks down her spine, and she almost dropped the baking sheet. "Oh... um...." *My hands are full. Just a sec. Coming right up.* "Right hand coming." *Oh my God, what did I just say?* "Shit! I meant, I'll be there in a minute."

Wolf chuckled in amusement. "It's okay, Jazz. I'm in no rush."

Jazz. He called me Jazz. Omigod, he knows my name! Her feet stuck to the floor with magic shoe glue, making her few steps to the espresso machine more like a stiff shuffle. "Um… sure. Madge should be back soon."

"What if I didn't come in to see Madge?"

Jazz's heart flipped over, dropped to her toes, and then tangoed back up to her chest. "Um… I guess you want your usual latte?" She packed the portafilter and thankfully slipped it into place without dropping grounds all over the counter. She reached for the milk in the fridge. "Bill isn't coming over today. Madge said he had a bad night. That's why she's getting him set up at home. He can't do his tanks so well." *Gah! Stop spitting out word salad!*

"I came in to get my coffee and Danish fix. To go, please. Mind if I ask you something?"

"Sure." Jazz popped the top off the plastic jug and filled the metal pitcher. Her heart was pounding. Wolf seldom looked at or addressed her for anything more than fulfilling his coffee order. She was still in awe that he knew her name.

"What do you know about computer scams, phone scams, that sort of thing?"

That brought her up short. Milk sloshed over her hand as she jolted. In her surprise, she forgot to be awkward. "I... uh... some. Why?"

"Do you happen to be called Jazzyhands online?"

Eep! How do I handle this? "That's one of my names," she said with caution. The milk frothed under the steam as the machine spat out its fragrant goodness. "I sometimes mess around with scammers. You know, keep them on the phone, screw up their schtick." *Mess up their computers by dropping viruses, erase their data, steal back what they took from so many good, unsuspecting people when I can.* "That sort of thing."

"I need to thank you."

The pretty leaf pattern she'd formed at the top of his cup became a blob as she miscalculated the pour. She was sure her face flushed red, making it appear blotchy and totally unattractive. "Thank me? For what?"

His eyes captured hers, and the breath in her chest became still.

"Do you remember a woman named Delia Best?"

"Um... yeah?"

"She's my landlady. She told me a girl by the

name of Jazzyhands kept her from making a mistake and losing a bunch of money to some phone scam thing. Delia said this Jazzyhands girl lives in this neighborhood and works for Madge and Bill. It didn't take me long to figure out that it had to be you."

Jazz coughed to cover her surprise and handed him a white paper cup and a full bag. "Yeah, well, I'm pretty good with computer skills and know my way around a code or two. I'm glad to help where I can. You know Madge and Bill lost a lot of money that way." She shrugged. "Makes me so angry when people are taken advantage of like that."

He took the cup and lightly brushed her fingertips with his, zapping her with kinetic energy. "I want you to know, I appreciate what you did for her. Delia's been widowed a long time now and doesn't have family close by. She doesn't have a lot of money and rents the upper part of her house to make ends meet. I consider that woman to be under my protection and the protection of the club. Means something to me."

Jazz dropped her eyes and tried to hide her grin. "Oh... uh... well, I'm happy Delia is okay."

"You want to know what else?"

She swallowed the sudden pool that appeared on her tongue and hoped she wouldn't choke on her own spit. "What?"

He leaned in, and those gorgeous eyes of his held her in place like predator and prey.

"I consider you under my protection and the club's protection now. Take care, Jazz."

Jazz's brain short-circuited as she watched her favorite biker leave the bakery.

He knows my name, and I'm under his protection. Under his protection. Under his... omigod! How was she supposed to handle this new information? What did it mean?

Several scenarios flew through her head. Pictures of Wolf in all his biker glory, taking her out to a five-star restaurant and then a movie. Nope, that looked funny. How 'bout a trip to the zoo and then a fast-food joint? More likely, but still weird. Riding on his bike through the mountains? That spot was reserved for girlfriends. Did bikers have girlfriends, or was it old ladies like the romance books said?

"Yo! We gonna get our coffees or what?"

The customer's loud inquiry startled her from her fantasy world, and she jumped in surprise, yelping in pain when her elbow grazed the counter. The awkward movement made her phone drop from her apron pocket, and as luck would have it, the whole device exploded into pieces.

"Oh, poop." Jazz made a point of limiting her cuss

words at work, though she had no trouble letting loose at home. She bent to clean up the carnage as Madge blustered into the store.

"Mornin'," the woman greeted her hurriedly before donning her own apron and getting straight to work.

Jazz shook her head to get back on track. She slipped the pieces of her phone into the big front pocket and thought more about her encounter with Wolf. His protection probably meant that he'd keep an eye on her like he did Bill and Madge. That was a nice idea, and she should be satisfied with that. Sometimes it was best to appreciate the gifts that were given rather than ask for something impossible.

With that thought, Jazz smiled and thanked the universe for Wolf's recognition. Broken phone or not, hearing her favorite biker say her name was enough to make her day.

6

THE PRESSURE IN WOLF'S HEAD POUNDED IN tandem with the music. Harper ground away onstage, working the pole while Portia worked the crowd. Both women had bills stuffed under their sparkly thongs. Whistles, catcalls, and loud whoops added to the cacophony. Most nights the noise didn't bother him, but he'd woken up this afternoon with gritty eyes and a nasty migraine. Spring had dumped her annual load of tree pollen with dusty yellow clouds that coated everything. It was mainly the greenways at the river, as there weren't a lot of wooded areas in the city, but yesterday's trip had affected him the most.

He'd ridden his bike right through the thick haze in the budding mountains to Moundsville, West

Virginia. At least once a month, he visited the prison there to see Cesar Beltran, otherwise known as Go-Kart to the club. He was one of the few members who didn't work with the steel mills directly; rather, he rebuilt engines and did car mods and other custom work in the machine shop.

He'd been caught at a street racing event during a police raid. Normally, it would only be a two- or three-hundred-dollar fine; however, when the police showed up, the crowd panicked and ran into the street during one of the races. The drivers took action immediately, but making a four-thousand-pound vehicle go from 125 to 0 in seconds is physically impossible without someone getting hurt. Cesar skidded and avoided hitting anyone, but some of the other drivers weren't so lucky. Thankfully, no one died, but there were several injuries, including some children.

Instead of blaming the parents who brought their kids to a midnight street race, the cops rounded up as many drivers as they could find and charged them all with child endangerment. Cesar, being who he was and wearing club colors, ended up in prison, where he'd been for the past year.

Since Wolf didn't get his usual daytime rest yesterday, that threw off his pattern. He was working on roughly four hours of sleep in the last twenty-four. At one time in his life, he could go for days on very little sack time, but he was closer to forty than thirty, and the effects of aging had started to creep up on him.

"What's up, baby?" Candie walked up to him, her enhanced breasts bouncing with every step of her stilettos. The bra she wore barely contained the masses, and her nipples poked through, leaving nothing to the imagination.

"Same old, same old. Aren't you supposed to robe up before coming out to greet your fans?"

"I don't have anything to hide from my fans." She tittered and ran a sharp clawlike talon down his arm. "Besides, there's only one fan I want to greet. You doin' anything after?"

Wolf's dick twitched in automatic response to the invitation, but he shook his head. "No, thanks."

They had been off-and-on lovers over the years, but he never considered her seriously, nor she him. Candie had many men in her life and changed boyfriends frequently. Wolf had been fine with being the in-between for a while, but at this point in his life, he was tired of playing musical beds. If all he wanted was to get laid, he only had to crook his finger at one of the dancers and he'd be set. Candie's offer might have scratched an itch, but he had no desire for another empty encounter. No, the only female he found intriguing at this time was a part-time barista with blue hair.

The Iron City Knights didn't have a stable of prostitutes or maintain a club group of sweetbutts. None of the dancers were forced to sleep with the members to keep their jobs either, but many of them did by choice. If someone wanted a hookup, that was fine, but there was no requirement. Solicitation was forbidden at the strip club itself. However, some of the more entrepreneurial dancers offered services for hire from time to time. They took their clients to the cheap pay-by-the-hour motel a few streets over. Wolf believed that to be their own business, and as long as they kept that shit separate from the club, he turned a blind eye. Occasionally, one of them got in trouble and called the club. More than once, he'd gone over to rescue a dancer from a bad situation. Despite the hands-off policy, the club took care of its people.

Candie puffed out her bright red lips as she turned to leave. "You sure? If you change your mind, come find me."

"I will. Thanks."

His neck cramped, and the pain intensified with the music's volume. He pressed his fingers against his temples to try to find some relief. Candie started her show with a big dip, thighs spread wide as she humped the pole. The crowd's roar of approval sent spikes through his brain.

"Fuck," he muttered as he pressed the heel of one hand against his twitching right eye. "Yo, Camshaft. You got any painkillers?"

"Want a blunt? Melter's probably got some."

"Fuck no. That shit doesn't help."

"Bet he's got some blues or whites on him too."

Wolf rolled his uncovered eye toward the younger man, anger flashing in the single green orb. "Where the fuck is he getting fentanyl and oxycodone? Does Scrap know about this?"

Camshaft shook his head. "Nah, you got it wrong. He ain't dealin'. They're left over from his surgery last month when they did that fusion thing to his back." He shrugged. "Scrap wouldn't care anyway. He's not paying attention to much these days."

Another roar crashed into Wolf's ears, nearly sending him to his knees. Candie probably just shed her top, and the fucking jagoffs acted like they'd never seen a pair of tits before.

Fuck, fuck, fuck!

"Hey, you don't look too good."

"I'm not," Wolf bit out.

"It's a pretty standard night. Why don't you go home? We got this."

It wasn't in Wolf's nature to give in, but the pain in his head made him rethink that position. "Yeah, I'm outta here. Call me if something happens."

He opted to text Scrap instead of heading to the back exit to tell the club president he was leaving and that he'd update the club on Go-Kart at the next church meeting. Whenever that happened. Scrap seldom called membership meetings. At this point, Wolf wasn't sure if the charter even got renewed and registered to make them a club instead of a riding group. They had bylaws, but no one really followed them. Hell, the last time the whole group went on a long ride or to a rally was three summers ago. Nothing significant since.

His bike sat parked in the narrow back lot of the building. He'd have to go around the block to get to it, but he didn't want to wade through the crowd and take a chance on some fucker whooping in his face. He'd likely take him out with a roundhouse punch.

The cooler air, dark streets, and less noise seemed to help. Melter's free pill giveaway concerned him, but he'd deal with it another time. Right now, he just wanted to get home, take a handful of industrial-strength painkillers, and crawl into his bed.

The full helmet muffled the bike's rumble as he crossed the bridge and entered his neighborhood. He passed the greenway buffer to the river and was nearly at the bakery before he realized the route he'd followed on autopilot. He pulled over to the curb and checked his phone. Just after midnight. It would be hours before Madge opened the place for business. Too bad, as he was craving a Danish and a coffee. One with a creative leaf pattern on top.

His thoughts naturally drifted to the cute employee. He thought Jazz was probably a nickname or shortened version of something else. It surprised him that Delia had named her as the person who saved her from that phone scammer thing. He got a kick out of teasing the blue-haired girl, but there was more to the woman than he thought. She'd never made a big impression on him until now. Part hippie chick, part computer whiz, part internet Robin Hood, part bakery helper. He wondered what he would find if he peeled back more layers of her personality.

He had to pass Bill and Madge's place on the way to his own, and alarm flared in his gut to see the house lights blazing bright. It stood out along the dark row of other homes. Something wasn't right.

He pulled up to the front and cut the engine. The silence made his ears ring as he pulled off the helmet.

He unlocked his phone to send a text to Madge when it buzzed in his hand.

Must be providence, he thought. *Either that or the universe is fucking with me.* "Madge, what's wrong?"

She sounded breathless. "It's Bill. He fell, and I can't lift him. I can't call Jazzy, and she can't lift him anyway. He's in a lot of pain and still won't let me get an ambulance. I don't know who else can come out but you."

She seemed frantic and on the edge of losing it.

"Insurance doesn't cover that shit!" Bill yelled faintly in the background.

"You're in luck. I'm right outside your house."

Wolf leaned the bike on its stand and opened the squeaky gate to the cracked sidewalk. A dozen steps later, he stepped up onto the porch under the yellow bug light and knocked on their front door. Madge met him in a zipped-up housecoat and slippers, her hair sticking out in all directions and gray circles under her eyes. Exhaustion was written all over her face, and it wasn't hard to tell that she'd reached the end of her rope.

"Stupid, stubborn mule would rather stay on the floor all night than let me get help," she snapped.

Bill's gargling yell came from somewhere in the

house. "Dammit, Madge! I told you to leave him alone!"

Madge fired right back. "It needs done, ya jagoff!" She turned to Wolf. "Can you get him up and in the bed for me?"

"Yeah."

He brushed past her to find Bill sprawled on the floor of the hallway. Nothing was around for him to grasp or take his weight, which meant he'd have to deadlift the big man.

"Where's his wheelchair?" Wolf asked.

Madge hurried into the back to get it.

Bill grumbled and made noises of protest during the entire operation. "Damn nuisance. Pain in the ass. Useless."

Wolf couldn't tell if he referred to himself, his wife, or his rescuer. Either way, the pain that had simmered down in his head after he left the club came back to life with a vicious twist between his eyes. He almost dropped Bill as the man cursed again, this time in a pain that echoed the one in Wolf's head.

"Son of a bitch! I think I broke my gawddamn arm!"

Madge visibly paled. "That's it. I'm calling the ambulance."

"For Chrissake, woman! Just put me in the car and take me to the damn hospital. I don't want those damn sirens wailing through here, waking the neighbors and telling everyone our business!"

Madge opened her mouth to argue with her stubborn husband, then shut it with a click. Wolf agreed with her silent decision. Better to save her temper and get him medical treatment ASAP. "Wolf, can you put him in the car? I'll go get dressed and be down in a jiffy." She looked closer at the biker's face. "Whatsamatta with you?"

Wolf forced his mouth to relax. "I'm good. I'll follow you to the hospital."

Madge shook her head. "They got people there who can unload him. If you want to help me, can you go by Jazzy's place and tell her what's happened and that I need her to open the bakery for me? I don't know how long we'll be there, and my people need their morning cup."

"Give me her number and I'll text her."

"She broke her phone yesterday and needs buying one. Her place isn't far, just down the greenway on Butler." Madge rattled off the address. "Jazzy don't sleep much and does a lot of computer stuff at night. I'm sure she's still up even at this hour."

Wolf's eyes felt like they wanted to pop from their

sockets. Madge's focus on Bill kept her from noticing, but that was okay. Yeah, he'd go knock on Jazz's door and tell her what's going on, then get home himself and eat a bottle of Excedrin or Tylenol or both. Whatever he had in his cabinet. Shit, he hoped nothing had expired.

Madge's taillights went in one direction and Wolf's in another. He found Jazz's house and parked next to her car. He almost missed the odd-looking abode, as only the short bridge connecting it to the road was visible in the dark. He noticed the house faced the greenway and river, and he bet the views were fantastic.

Sure enough, he spotted the lights on in one upper room, just as Madge had said. Even if the house had been dark, he'd still have banged on the door, not caring about waking her. His goal was to get the message to the pretty barista and leave.

He knocked on the door as he swayed with a churning gut. Moments later, Jazz appeared. Her image swam in front of him, and his stomach flipped over as a ringing filled his ears, blocking out all other sound. *Fuck* was his last coherent thought as he let loose over the railing. *Way to impress a lady, asshole.*

He spat the foul taste from his mouth and garbled his words out quickly before his brain exploded.

"Madge took Bill to the emergency room and needs you to open the bakery for her."

The world tilted with sickening angles. Passing out seemed both imminent and a good idea. "Mind if I come in for a minute?"

Without waiting for her answer, he lumbered into her house in search of a place to collapse before he landed on the floor.

"My name is Mike, and I'm calling from the Internal Revenue Service. Are you aware you have unpaid taxes?"

Jazz coughed. Today she'd decided on her old woman persona. "Oh, dearest, I haven't paid any taxes since my husband died about seven years ago. He was the one who paid all our bills."

"I'm sorry to hear that, but you must pay something today or else we will have no choice but to send the authorities to arrest you. They're on their way now and will be there in thirty minutes if you don't."

Her fingers flew over the keyboard, easily hacking into her opponent's system. *Not much here. Must be a first-timer.*

In less than three minutes, she cleaned him out

and then dropped the facade. "All done, Sparky. I'd find some other line of work. You really suck at this one."

"Wha—"

She didn't wait for the guy to get his muddled brain in order. She closed off the call and scrubbed everything.

A few moments later, a message popped up on her computer.

> Copperpot100: I only took out three tonight. Pretty slim pickings. You?

> Jazzyhands: Just one. I've been pretty busy lately with work and the coffee shop.

Copperpot100 was one of the original scam-shielders, perhaps even the one who started the online team. No one had a clue if Copper was a man or a woman, and the anonymity of the online IDs was critical to their cause. Still, it was sometimes easy to guess the person behind the handle. Jazz had no idea how many members had joined this group of computer vigilantes, but everybody had only one goal: take out as many scammers and sites as possible. Jazz loved the phone call schemes and had dealt with fake Amazon and bank pages. Glyndathegood did well with the romance catfishers, the ones who sent pics of sexy men to lonely women and convinced them to give up their life savings for love. Bomber123 favored the charity email scams. Muscleman2019 took out business fraud. Copperpot100 did them all.

> Copperpot100: I wish I'd gotten online earlier. Too late for a woman in Ohio. Her credit card maxed out in seconds.

Jazz picked up her half-eaten hoagie and took a huge bite, grateful she didn't have her webcam on. This time of night, she wore her most torn-up LuLaRoe leggings and a holey gray thermal. No bra as she was home and only wore one when she left it. The house was cool but not uncomfortably so. The proximity to the river and the winds from the moving waters kept it cool enough at night that she didn't need air-conditioning most of the time, and the summer heat was still a long way off.

> Jazzyhands: Jeez, that sucks donkey balls.

> Copperpot100: LMFAO!

She grinned and shifted the food from one side of

her cheek to the other. Freya jumped onto the desk and started sniffing at the Darth Vader-shaped plate. "Get off, ya freeloader."

Copperpot100: I saw on the dark web about a hacker who took down an entire network and its partner networks. Know anything about that?

Jazz grinned around her full mouth and typed with one hand.

Jazzyhands: Not a thing, but I bet it was epic.

Copperpot100: Epic is one word. Dangerous is another. From the scuttlebutt out there, the network systems were linked to some transportation tracking systems. An entire airline got crippled by that virus, leaving planes unable to fly. It also crashed the navigation for train travel systems in three countries. No major accidents, but it stranded people for hours. Cost that company millions.

Jazz paused with the sandwich halfway to her open mouth. The thought hadn't occurred to her that the trouble she caused might hurt the very people she wanted to protect. She took another bite and rapidly typed as she chewed.

Jazzyhands: If it's the virus I'm thinking of, then it has special markers to protect legit code. Pretty tricky stuff, but if the scammers are connected to legit businesses, like for laundering the scammed funds, then there's bound to be some crossover. I'm sure whoever let that virus loose didn't mean anything bad.

Copperpot100: I have no doubts about the person who designed and released that virus. I hope they will be more careful in the future.

Why did she feel as if she'd been scolded by an older brother? She dug her bare toes into the thin rug at her feet and switched the subject.

Jazzyhands: Guess what?

Copperpot100: What?

Jazzyhands: Remember that biker guy I told you about? The one with the cool hair and great body?

Copperpot100: Yeah, what about him?

> Jazzyhands: HE SPOKE TO ME AND EVEN CALLED ME BY NAME!!

> Copperpot100: Slow down, cowgirl. You do know biker gangs are a pretty rough crowd. I wouldn't want you to get involved with those kinds of criminals.

> Jazzyhands: Biker CLUB, not GANG. Besides, he's a good biker. Not a bad one.

> Copperpot100: There's a difference?

> Jazzyhands: Of course!

A hard pounding on the door caught her attention. Only one person would dare come see her in the middle of the night.

> Jazzyhands: I gotta go. My sister just showed up. She probably needs money again. Bleh, I wish she'd get a clue that I'm as broke as she is! TTFN!

She logged off before Copperpot responded and took another huge bite of her sandwich. "I'm comin', jerkface!" she yelled around the gargantuan mass before stomping as loudly as her bare feet allowed to the back street door. "If you need money, you'll have to hit up Hugo 'cause you still owe me from last mo—"

Her voice died as Wolf filled the door. He squinted at her, somewhat unsteady on his feet.

Oh shit! Are you drunk? What are you doing here? How did you find me? "Doing me drunk?" *Dammit! I wish the earth would open up and swallow me whole!*

Wolf just looked at her. Then he groaned and leaned over the railing as he vomited into the bushes.

7

THE LIGHT SCENT OF LAVENDER TEASED HIS nostrils, and he inhaled deep. It came from the cloud of soft hair in front of him. He floated somewhere between waking and sleeping but still became aware of the lithe body he spooned.

It was not his room or his house. He could tell that much, although he had no clue of his location. It was very rare that he spent a whole night in someone else's bed, but apparently he had. There was a vague memory of lifting Bill off the floor, but after that, he drew a blank.

The woman in front of him stirred and pressed her bottom against his morning wood. The ache in his dick made him wonder how far they went. Must not have been very far if he was still hard and horny, not to mention he had no memory of being inside a woman last night. The room was dark, so he couldn't see which dancer ended up in bed with him.

He swept his hand upward along a smooth rib cage, taking the sleep shirt with it. A small breast settled nicely in his hand, and he rolled the nipple into a point with his thumb. The softness of a natural breast without any enhancement filled his palm, so not Candie, thank God. Ellie had been making eyes and dropping hints lately. She was on the cusp of being too young for him, but perhaps he'd given in last night and taken her up on her offer. The woman let out a sleepy groan and arched, rubbing against his hard dick, both teasing and encouraging.

That was all he needed to push her shoulder to the bed and take that nipple into his mouth. He curled his tongue around the tight nub and slid his hand across to tease the other one. The gasp she made when he sucked it rang in his ears like music.

He kept up his ministrations for a minute before sliding his hand down her taut abdomen and into her panties. Why she had on any clothes in the first place confused him. Getting dressed after sex meant leaving, not spending the night. His fingers encountered crisp hair as they found their mark.

He yanked his hand back and nearly fell from the

bed. Not one stripper at the club kept a full bush, and most shaved themselves bare. Hell, Candie even had hers lasered permanently. Who the fuck?

A reading light clicked on, one of those older ones that clamped onto a headboard. Jazz lay in front of him, clutching a quilt to her chin and eyeing him warily.

"Um... hi, Wolf." Her voice squeaked as she greeted him.

Fuck, fuck, fuck, fuck! *What did I do last night?* "Jazz." What was he supposed to say now? "Look, I'm sorry for...." *For what?* "Uh, why am I here?"

"You came to tell me about Bill and Madge being at the hospital." The statement came from the cloth bundle. "Then you stumbled into my house and passed out on the bed. You told me you had a massive headache before you went down. I gave you an Imitrex injection. I get migraines, too, from time to time and have a stash on hand for when it happens. I hope that was okay."

Wolf jammed his hands through his hair, noticing for the first time that his shirt was off, but he still had on his pants. He cleared his throat. "Jazz, did I... do anything to you?"

She shook her head. "Nothing like that happened." He watched as her face turned a peachy shade of red. "At least, not... uh... like I said, you passed out. My sofa isn't great to sleep on, so I thought I'd stay in my bed, too, and just wake up before you did. I guess I miscalculated. Sorry about that."

Fuck, I'm the one who assaulted her, and she's sorry? "There's nothing you need to be sorry about, Jazz. I'm the one who fucked up. I was still half asleep when I put my hands on you, but that's no excuse. I hope you'll forgive me."

"I forgive you, okay? I gotta get going to the bakery before I'm late."

Wolf heard the desperate hint in her voice. "I'll get out of your hair, then. See ya."

He snatched his shirt from the floor and pulled the Henley over his head. "Thanks. Again." His reply was awkward and lame as hell, but he couldn't think of anything else to say. The keys to his bike jingled reassuringly in his pocket as he bolted from the house.

JAZZ BLEW THE BANGS OFF HER FACE AS SHE dumped two portafilters at the same time. The line was still thick, but the people in it were waiting patiently for her to make their morning cup, hand it to them along with a pastry, and then collect their money. One person serving what looked like a bazillion, and she was rushing as fast as she could, all the while answering the repeated question of "Where's Madge?"

This was actually good, as it didn't give her any time to think about the early morning's events.

It didn't take her long to figure out what had happened last night. Wolf wasn't drunk—he was in pain. His scrunched-up face was a big clue. Also his fingers pressing into his forehead and temples. Classic pressure points to relieve headaches. He delivered his message about Bill's fall and potential injuries, and Madge needing her to cover the morning rush solo. Then he seemed to forget where he was and staggered into her bedroom to collapse on the bed. She'd brought him one of her pills and found him already passed out cold with his shirt off. This was abnormal, as migraines usually kept someone awake, but maybe Wolf was different. She watched him for several minutes as she debated on giving him an injection. It probably wasn't ethical at all, but he was writhing in pain, so she decided it was better to ask forgiveness than permission.

Jazz packed both filters, slipped them into place,

and started the machine, double shots on either side. The steamer hissed as she started frothing the milk. For no particular reason, a picture of Wolf in all his tattooed glory across her bed came into her mind. Damn, if her phone had been working, she might have snuck a picture of that. Not to share, just to keep and look at from time to time. He didn't have one specific large piece, just a lot of smaller ones. A howling wolf on his left pec and a detailed moon on the other. A picture of a large black bird perched on a skull across his stomach with its spread wings hugging him around to his back. A plain cross surrounded by roses on his forearm. One of his nipples held a small gold ring. Everywhere she had looked, there was a piece of art on his body.

Another customer walked in to join the crowd. "Be with you in a minute!" Jazz yelled as she dumped and stirred. Most of these were to go, so they didn't get the fancy coffee art she usually did for the ones who stayed in the shop.

She turned with two paper cups in her hands and nearly collided with Wolf. Apparently, he was the newcomer and had come behind the counter before she saw him.

He took the cups from her and handed them off

to the waiting customer. "Didja order a pastry? Which one?"

Omigod, he's here. What do I say? "Happy you're here"? "Thanks for coming"? "Happy coming." Shit! Really, Jazz?

"You'll have to show me how to work the register." He ignored her odd word choices and handed the guy at the counter a white bag of treats. "And you're almost out of baklava."

"Um… okay." Jazz turned away from him and started another four shots. The machine spit out its caffeinated goodness, and she mixed more lattes. A few patrons wanted straight up brewed coffee, and Wolf took care of them. Between the two of them, the morning rush was served and out the door. The ones coming in now were the day-timers, older men and women who didn't have jobs or places to be but didn't want to stay at their houses. Jazz took a pot of coffee and went out to top off a table of old men who sat pontificating on how the city used to be different and updating one another on their daily activities.

"My car needs cleaning this weekend. I'm taking her to that new detail place in Sharpsburg."

"Stillers got a new quarterback this season."

"The trial started for that guy who tried to rob the Green Street Bank last year."

Jazz wiped a table down as she recalled that event. Three men entered the old bank with the intent of taking as much cash as they could carry, but they ended up in an hours-long police standoff. Shots were fired, and a couple of people were killed and even more hurt, including one of the Iron City Knights. Quillon was the name Wolf said when he told Madge and Bill about it. From what she remembered, Quillon saved one of the tellers by diving on top of her and even took a bullet to the leg. They were an item now.

If a bank teller and a biker can make a solid couple, how 'bout a barista and a biker?

She shook her head to clear the wayward thought. *Not possible. You can't even talk straight around the man, let alone date him.*

"Jazz."

"Gah!"

The unexpected voice behind her made her jump three feet into the air. Her balance tilted, and she almost fell on her ass. A pair of thick arms caught her, and once again, she found herself in the embrace of the man she drooled over. The man who woke her up this morning by—

Lalala! Don't go there, Jazz! Her mental admonition didn't help. Both nipples tightened into prominent points, and she prayed they didn't show.

"Easy, baby. I didn't mean to scare you."

Oooooh! He called me baby!

"I'm good. Just... good."

"Here." He placed an Android phone box in her hand as he guided her behind the counter. "It's not the latest model, but it's new, and it works. I'm assuming you'll be able to use it with whatever carrier you're on. I wrote my number on the side. Once you have it, program me in and text me so I have yours, yeah?"

Jazz was stunned. *How did you know my phone got fucked up? Thanks for thinking of me. I'll get it straight.* "Fuck me straight." *Shit!* "I mean... thinks for thanking." *No!* "Thanks for me." *Ugggh! Can I please die now?*

He chuckled at her mixed-up words but didn't tease her about them. "Madge called. Bill didn't break his arm."

She smiled in relief. "Oh, that's good news. I hope they'll be home soon." She ticked off her fingers one by one. "We need more than just baklava made. There's Long Johns and cinnamon rolls, too, plus—"

He held up a hand, palm out, interrupting her baked goods inventory list. "Hold up. Like I said, he didn't break his arm. He broke two ribs, his collarbone, and cracked his shoulder blade."

Her stomach bubbled with sudden dread. "Oh shit."

"Yeah. Madge is gonna need a lot of help for a while."

"I'm only part-time, because... well... they can't afford to pay me more. I'll work as much as she'll let me, though."

He frowned. "How can you live on part-time work?"

"I have another job?"

"Is that a question?"

"I have another job."

He leaned on the counter and regarded her with his glowing eyes. "What else do you do besides make coffee?"

"I created the inventory database system for Steelworks Inc. They pay me monthly to maintain it and take care of any problems if it crashes. I have it to the point that it's pretty self-reliant and will alert me if anything goes down."

One of his eyebrows arched. "That's impressive. You're a smart woman. You went to college for that?"

Jazz felt her cheeks heat. "Yes, but my major was graphics and programming, not software engineering.

I graduated and... well... just happened to find this field." *Yeah, "happened" because of Madge and Bill, Delia, and a whole lotta other folks just like them.*

He stood up from his position and regarded her with those gorgeous eyes of his. "So, messin' with scammers is just a side thing? You don't make money with it?" His easy posture sent her libido into overdrive.

She pressed her lips together and got a firm grip on her hormones. She reached down and pulled an empty tray from the display case, keeping her eyes on her task. "Nope. Some people have monetized it by making YouTube videos and contests from the phone calls, but no one I know takes money from victims. The bottom line is, we do what we do to help people. Like your landlady."

He frowned and took the heavy metal sheet from her hands. "We? There are more than just you?"

Her grin returned. "There's a network of people who take on scammers, bots, fake accounts, all sorts of stuff. It's sad we have to do this, but...."

"But what?"

Jazz turned to Wolf and, for the first time, stood tall and met his eyes directly. "I've had too many people I know personally who were targeted by those criminals. I've seen people get taken for a few hundred, others for a few thousand. Then there are the ones like Madge and Bill. They lost their entire savings on an online retirement investment company that turned out to be a scam." She raised her fists and flared her fingers. "Poof. Just like that, a lifetime of work, gone. By the time they figured it out, their money had disappeared into cyberspace, and there was nothing they could do about it. Bill spent his life pouring steel at the forge and ended up broke and disabled. The only income they have left is what the bakery produces. They should be retired at their age, but they can't afford it now. It's not right, and I have the ability to do something about it. Part of that is making coffee and helping them around here. The other part is using my talent to shield vulnerable people when I can. That's what we unofficially call ourselves—scam-shielders."

"That's really cool." His approving smile sent thrills from her head to her toes, making her movements tight and jerky. She popped off one portafilter, fumbled it, and spilled grounds all over the counter. Her cheeks flamed at his amused chuckle.

"You guys got a website? How do people find you?"

She scooped the mess into her hand and turned away to dump it into the trash bin. "We don't advertise or sell our services. We're just a bunch of people who get together online sometimes and kick some scammer ass. We get hundreds of bogus emails and texts every day. That makes it easy to find them when we have time. It's not like we have work hours." The bell rang as a few more customers came in. "Although, I think I'm gonna message some of them later and let them know I'll be off-grid for a while. I believe I'm gonna be needed here more in the next weeks, and I still have my day job to handle."

Wolf stood directly behind her. "Yeah, I'd say you're right. I'll be stepping in as needed too." His voice got serious, dropping in volume and pitch. "Listen, I don't want this to get awkward between us over what happened this morning. I repeat, I'm sorry for touching you like I did, and I hope you won't hold that against me."

I really do want to hold it against you. I mean me. I want to hold me against you just for a minute. Jazz pressed her lips together to keep from speaking. No way did she want to screw up her words this time. No telling what embarrassing phrase would come out.

He must have taken her silence as anger. "Look, we're gonna need to get through this so we can work together."

She thought carefully before she replied. "I get it.

I'm okay working with you as long as you're okay working with me?"

"Is that another question?"

Jazz took a big breath before turning to face him. *I can control my mouth. I can control my thoughts. I can control my hormones.* "I'm okay working with you as long as you're okay working with me."

He chuckled again at her carefully worded sentence. "Good. Now show me how to use the register properly."

8

Lynn Farthing pulled at the boning in the tight corset underneath her dress as she entered the Radisson West Hotel. The upscale resort was a far cry from the tiny one-bedroom apartment she barely afforded. Rent was disgustingly high in this part of California, and her job as a high school guidance counselor didn't pay all the bills. The divorce settlement she got from her ex-husband helped, but it was still hard for her to make ends meet. At age fifty, she was essentially starting over.

Her best friend at the school had turned her onto this dating app. More like a hookup app, as most of the people there were looking for a temporary sex partner. Lynn figured if her ex used the app, she had that option as well.

The bar was tasteful and high-class. Lynn felt frumpy and way too old to be there, but she'd taken the train into the city and was determined to follow through with this... meeting? Assignation? Fucking?

She raised a hand to her freshly colored blonde hair and glanced at the picture on her phone. Gilbert was the only name he gave. His profile said he was a marketing consultant for the travel business and somewhat younger than her. For what reason he swiped on her profile, she did not know. What were the chances that he liked older women?

Older. Fatter. Overworked. She shook her head. This was not about any future plans. This was just about getting laid, and somehow she needed to let her ex find out about it. He got himself a pretty little fuck toy, so she could, too, right?

One last look at the picture, and she slipped the phone in her purse. She scanned the room.

"CatLady50?" A deep male voice vibrated near her left ear.

Shit-oh-shit-oh-shit! Lynn swallowed and steeled herself before she turned to face the man. "Yes, it's nice to meet yoooo... *oh my.*"

Stunning dark eyes peered down at her from the handsomest face she'd seen in a long time—high cheekbones, strong jawline with a close sculpted beard, long nose. The only mar was a small scar in front of his left ear and a light smattering of gray at his temples. He dressed in a tailored business suit and gave off an aristocratic vibe. The aura he exuded was as powerful and wide as his shoulders, and she had no doubts that the rest of him would be as equally appealing naked as it was clothed.

What the fuck have I gotten myself into? "I'm sorry. This was a mistake. Have a nice night."

She slipped off the stool, but his hand on her forearm stopped her. "Did I upset you? Whatever I did, please accept my apology."

His tone was like velvet, and she wanted to hear more. "No, no, nothing like that. I'm just... I got divorced recently, and I thought I was ready for"— she gestured between them—"for this, but it's too much too soon."

If he had gotten mad at her, yelled or cursed at her, that would have been easy. She would have flipped him off and left. Instead, he gave a sigh that sounded defeated and nodded. "I understand. I lost my wife a year ago, and I'm still not over it yet. I'm sorry for wasting your time."

He sounded so genuine, sympathy hit her heart. "I'm so sorry for your loss. It must be hard."

He gave her a sad smile that made him even more

handsome. "It is sometimes. I'm on the road so much for work, and it gets lonely. I thought this app would help me to meet people and start healing, but...." He shrugged with his unfinished sentence.

Lynn swallowed her previous intentions. "Well, since you're here, why don't we have a drink? Just talk for a little while."

He smiled, showing incredibly white teeth. "Would you mind if we move to a booth? It's a little more private that way."

One drink turned into several. She told him about her husband—ex-husband now—cheating on her with a younger woman in his law firm. Gilbert asked about her work at the school. She mentioned her cats taking over her apartment, but she wouldn't give them up no matter what. "I have four, and they've been with me through the whole ordeal."

He talked about his job in hotel marketing, extensive travel, and how he wished he could be at home with his children. "My parents take care of them now. I want to be there for them, as they're still grieving for their mother, but it's impossible with my job, and I can't do anything about it. I've looked for something else, but I can't find one that pays like this one."

Lynn couldn't help but stare at his full lips as he spoke. He was such a nice man and sounded like a good father and was a good husband. Loving, faithful, kind, sexy as hell.

"I'm sorry this didn't work out. You really are a beautiful woman, and I'm very glad to have met you. May I walk you to your car?"

"I took the metro tonight, but we can go walk around the square outside for a bit before I leave."

"That would be lovely."

The Southern California night was clear and warm. Gilbert took her hand as they left the restaurant and walked outside the tall building. The sounds of the city surrounded them as they strolled. Lynn marveled at Gilbert's easy manner. He didn't let go of her hand, keeping it in a firm grip as they walked. Each time she glanced at him, he returned her gaze with a gentle smile. It had been such a long time since a man paid this kind of attention to her. What would it be like to be with him? As in *be* with him? That was why she was here, right?

As they circled back to the hotel, he lifted their joined fingers and pressed a soft kiss to the back of her hand. "I realize you have to go, but is there any possibility that you'd like to come up for a little while? Perhaps look at the stars from my balcony?"

Lynn hesitated. Going up to the man's room to see

stars wasn't the only invitation she heard. "Are you sure?"

His eyes darkened, and Lynn's breath caught with the burn she saw in them. "Absolutely."

He started kissing her in the elevator. Gentle at first, then with increased hunger. By the time they got into his room, she was breathless. He started pulling her clothes off as they stumbled through the suite and had her stripped to her panties by the time he got them to the bedroom. Lynn gasped as he pushed her flat to the mattress with her legs draped over the edge and yanked the last barrier down her thighs. "I've never done this before. A one-night stand that is."

He grinned as he knelt between her legs. "Then let's make it memorable." His mouth descended.

Lynn cried out as he drove her to orgasm without mercy. Even after she came the first time, he kept eating her until she climaxed again. Only after she came a third time did he relent. He stood up and shed his own clothes, revealing a tight masculine body. Sleek muscles, lines across his flat stomach, broad chest, and even a nipple ring.

Magnificent was her only thought as he rolled on a condom. She glanced at her stomach and made to put her hands over the loose skin.

Gilbert stopped her by drawing them away. He

pushed his hips between her generous thighs and placed her arms above her head as he came down on her body. "No, beautiful. Don't hide this from me."

"I'm a little self-conscious about my age, and—oh!"

He'd found his mark and slid inside her wet pussy in one firm stroke. "Does that feel like I care about our age difference?"

"No," she gasped as he moved in and out of her. She didn't think she could climax again, but it was definitely going to happen. He drove her to it with long, steady, precise strokes that showed no mercy as they brought her to another orgasm. His words washed over her as he moved. "Come with me, baby. *Mere priya.* My beautiful Lynn. Show me. Come. Come now."

She bowed up as she came screaming his name. He slammed into her harder and harder until he joined her, voicing his own release, and then collapsed on top of her. Lynn took his weight and ran her palms over his slick back. Her body hummed with a satisfaction she hadn't felt in a long time. It was unexpected and really, *really* nice.

"I haven't made love to a woman since my wife died," he confessed. "Thank you, my love. You have no idea how much this means to me." He kissed her sweetly and nuzzled her cheek. "Would it be too much to ask if we can take a bath together?"

She smiled and nodded at him. He smiled back and winked at her as he left the bed to go prepare in the bathroom. He didn't bother to get dressed or cover himself, and she watched his smooth buttocks flex as he walked away. It took everything in her not to squeal like one of the teenage girls she counseled. Never had sex been so fulfilling. So thorough. She felt like she was floating above the clouds. Gilbert was everything she'd ever wanted in a man.

The snarky part of her wished her ex's fuck toy good luck in getting the same thing. After twenty-five years of being with Gerald, she knew his standard-operational-procedure sex was completed in five to ten minutes, and once he was done, he was done. That was also after taking a little blue pill. Lynn smirked at the idea of her ex seeing her now, naked and being fucked deliciously by a man fifteen years or so her junior.

The water was just hot enough for a long soak. He helped her step into the tub and then pulled her to rest against him, her back to his front.

"Push the button, *priya*."

A moment later, a low hum started as the jets came awake, bubbling into the tub. Lynn relaxed and let herself fall into an afterglow languor. His hands roamed over her body, cupping her breasts and teasing her nipples into peaks. She saw his movements in the mirror directly across from them, and the sight was mesmerizing. She felt wanton and wanted, something she'd been craving since before her divorce.

"This has been a wonderful night," he murmured against her neck. "The best one I've had in a very long time."

"Do you think we can see each other again while you're in the city?"

He sighed as he gathered her hands together in one of his, crossing them over her chest and holding her in a tight hug. "I wish I could, beautiful, but unfortunately, I leave tomorrow morning. I have a job to finish first, and I promised my boss I would make it quick."

"What job is that?" she asked lazily, still watching him in the mirror.

His reflected eyes turned sad. "This."

He pushed her under the water and held her there until she stopped moving.

9

Jazz bent over to sweep the small pile of debris into the dustpan, and when she stood back up, several bones in her back popped like tiny firecrackers. It had been two weeks since Bill's fall. His level of cantankerousness was through the roof, but she understood that he was miserable. His lungs were already shot, and the pain of deep breathing exercises to heal his ribs made it worse. Any range of movement he'd had was even more restricted now, and he already hated the dependence he had on his wife for everything.

The daily routine was Jazz opening the bakery and coffee shop in the morning for the big rush, with Wolf joining her as soon as he could. Then Wolf went over to the house to sit with Bill while Madge came over to bake whatever needed replenishing and watch the shop while Jazz worked her day job for a few hours using the bakery's Wi-Fi. Then Jazz would go back to working the counter until closing at six, and Madge went home to relieve Wolf to give him a few hours of sleep before he had to be at the Attic. Sometimes, Jazz stayed later to finish baking what Madge started and then work her other job until her eyes wouldn't stay open. Mercifully, most of the inventory system she'd created was self-maintaining and only required a tweak or two to keep it up-to-date.

Wash. Rinse. Repeat.

Only a few more hours until closing, but she was wearing down quickly. Thankfully, there was a time limit to all the extra work. At least she hoped so.

She'd messaged Copperpot about her situation and that she would be out of the loop for the foreseeable future. He'd asked if she needed help and said he'd be glad to ride up to see her. She politely declined and wondered what he meant by "ride up." Everyone who was part of the scam-shielders was totally anonymous in name, location, and most of the time, gender. From some of Copperpot's messages, she got the impression that particular cohort was male. Maybe that phrase was just a colloquial saying in Copperpot's part of the country.

If he was even *in* the country. She was pretty sure Bomber123 was Canadian.

The door opened, and her sister entered pushing a stroller. Two other small children followed her, clamoring loudly about donuts.

"I want jelly!"

"I want a face one!"

Liz snapped at both of them, "Pipe down or you won't get anything!" She turned to Jazz. "Come by when you get off work, yeah? I need a break from the kids, and Mom said she's too busy."

"Hi, Liz. I'm afraid I can't. I'm working some serious overtime hours for the next few weeks and maybe longer. Can you get Leo to help you?"

Her sister scoffed as she flopped onto the closest chair, the legs scooting across the floor. "Yeah, right." The baby woke with a wail at the loud scraping sound. Instead of picking him up, Liz started jerking the stroller back and forth. It didn't help.

Jazz glanced nervously at the frowning patrons. There weren't too many this time of the day, but the ones who did come were looking for a quiet place to have a coffee and get some work done. Eric Nietz was in his usual spot with his laptop open. Jennifer Morrans was grading papers on the opposite side of the shop. Both had their eyes on the disturbances in the form of rambunctious children.

"Listen, Ian and Ivan, if you want donuts, I'll get them for you, but you have to sit still and be quiet, yeah?" Jazz told her nephews.

Ian climbed up onto the chair next to his mother, and Jazz lifted Ivan into a booster seat. Both of them had enough sense to settle down, and she hoped it stayed that way.

She hurried behind the counter and pulled out three donuts: a jelly, a clown face, and a chocolate glazed. Two cups of milk and one coffee later, the kids and Liz were content. The crying stopped when Liz plugged a bottle into the baby's mouth. Jazz took over, lifting the infant and cradling him while swaying from side to side despite her protesting back. "Mom and Dad doing okay?" she asked.

"Mom's pissed about the roof leaking again. The contractor said it needs re-shingled years ago, but she didn't want to spend money on it. Dad said he'd do another patch job. I told him not to bother, as it won't hold up any better than the last one."

Jazz's lower spine started to seize. She kept up her swaying so little Isaac would fall asleep and maybe she could put the child back into the stroller. "Why won't they get it done right?"

Liz slurped from the white mug and waved her hand in annoyance. "Too damn cheap. That house will fall apart before they drop a penny on proper upkeep. You coming for Easter dinner next weekend?"

Jazz made the transfer back to the stroller, and thankfully Isaac stayed asleep. "I don't know."

Liz frowned. "Mom will freak if you don't show up. She's expecting you."

Jazz arched her back to relieve the pressure on her spine. The bell over the door rang, and she spoke over her shoulder without turning. "Be right with you." To Liz she asked, "Will Leo be there?"

Liz rolled her eyes as she drained the cup. "No. Stupid jagoff left me again. I don't know where he's gone this time. Fucker comes home when the court starts chasing him for child support, then takes off when he's caught up."

Jazz didn't blame Leo much, although she thought he needed to step up as a father to his children. Ian, the oldest, had a different father, and Liz had never named him. Jazz was sure it was because her sister didn't really know exactly who impregnated her when she was just out of high school. Leo had come into the picture and helped make Ivan and Isaac.

Over the years, Liz—she hated being called Eliza-beth—had grown more and more like their mother, bitterly complaining about her lot in life. Leo hung on as long as he could, but Liz's constant nagging and demands for more had the potential to wear down a saint. The fights they got into turned into epic battles. One such episode recently happened on their parents' front lawn. Leo apparently started seeing someone on the side, and when Liz found out, all hell broke loose. She screamed obscenities at him and threw his stuff out the door. Leo lost his shit and yelled back about how her never-ending demands, relentless criticisms, and regular put-downs had driven him to this point. Nothing was ever good enough for her. Not his job. Not his clothes. Not his plans for the future. Not his family. Throughout the few years they'd been married, he would leave for a few weeks, then return until Liz chased him off again. Jazz was afraid this was the last time, as papers had been filed.

She changed the subject before Liz started on her exhaustive list of Leo grievances. "Have you talked to Hugo lately? He got moved to shift manager."

Liz scoffed. "He makes dog treats, for Chrissakes."

That pissed Jazz off. "He's an adult with Down syndrome who's highly functional and living on his own. So what if he works at a dog treat bakery and stays in a group home? He supports himself, and now he's in charge of other adults living with disabilities who work there. I think we should be proud of him and happy for him."

"He doesn't want to come home for Easter either. I don't know whatsamatta with you two. Can't visit your family once in a while."

I don't want to hear about my single state. Hugo doesn't want to hear about his decision to move out from under Mom's thumb. We both don't want to listen to who bitches more, you or Mom. "The group home probably had something going on, and he's helping with it."

Ivan spilled his milk on the table and started splashing it around. Liz moved only to lift her coffee mug. "Get me a refill when you fetch a towel, wouldja?"

Taking the mug, Jazz stepped back into a wall and nearly fell.

A large wall.

A large, hard wall.

A large, hard, hot wall.

Wolf grabbed her upper arms and steadied her, holding her back against his front. "I'll get the towels. You get the refill, yeah?"

"Um... okay." Jazz froze, unable to move.

Liz's eyes popped wide as they observed the man standing so close behind her sister. "Is *he* the reason you're not coming over for Easter?"

Ian stood up on his chair. "Are you Auntie J's boyfriend?"

Jazz's whole body jerked at the child's innocent question. *Just a coworker this week. He's a friend.* "Co-friend." *Dammit!*

Ian cocked his head in confusion. "What's a co-friend?"

Wolf answered as if he was used to translating Jazz-speak. "Friend and coworker. I'm helping out around the bakery until the owners get back on their feet. Now put your butt back in the chair." He turned to Liz. "Jazz hasn't told you about Madge and Bill?"

She snorted. "Jazz never tells us anything." Her eyes turned speculative, and her tone changed as if a switch had been flipped. "How old are you?"

Jazz noted the difference, and so did Wolf by the way his hands tightened on her arms.

"Thirty-six. Let's get this mess cleaned up, yeah?"

Jazz spurred into movement at Wolf's growl and pulled away from his grasp. "I'll get the mop."

Wolf wiped off the table while Jazz poured another cup of coffee before tackling the floor. Out of the corner of her eye, she watched her sister ask

Wolf questions as he worked. Even though they were too low to hear, Jazz had a good idea of what they were.

"What do you do for a living?"

"Married?"

"You got kids?"

"You got a house?"

The flirty look on Liz's face told Jazz her sister might be on the prowl for the next man in her life. Jazz couldn't blame her, as Wolf was a top male specimen, handsome and built like a tank. To Liz, every man was a potential partner, and they were all interested in her. Jazz had heard her give this particular interview many times, and she wondered if Liz had been as faithful in her marriage as she expected Leo to be. It bugged the snot out of her that Liz held her husband to one standard while she herself felt free to do whatever.

What was worse? The idea that Liz had an eye on Wolf, the same man Jazz had been secretly crushing on for years.

Whatever answers Wolf gave made Liz frown. He nodded and turned to walk away, facing Jazz at the counter, and his eyes met hers. For a split second, they stared at each other, and then he did something she never thought she'd see.

He rolled them. Actually rolled his eyes about her sister.

Ha! Jazz's throat quivered with restrained laughter, and she had to bite her lip to keep it from bursting out. The cup overflowed, and she wiped the spill with a rag before returning to the table. "Here ya go. Fresh brewed and hot."

Liz opened her mouth to vent whatever displeasure she had, but Wolf called from the back kitchen where he'd retreated. "Jazz, I need you back here."

"Coming."

She hurried to find Wolf leaning on the work counter with his arms crossed and a wry smile on his face. "You owe me."

Jazz blinked. "I owe you?"

"Is that a question?"

"Actually, it is. How do I owe you?"

Wolf straightened and put his hands in his pockets. Jazz's gaze was drawn to the Iron City Knights logo on his black leather cut, a longsword with a rounded handguard through a grinning skull. She'd already memorized their motto: "Through the fires of hell, men of steel are forged."

"Your sister is a piece of work. My ex-wife wasn't that bad."

Jazz tried to wrap her head around this new information. "You... you were married?"

"Yeah. For about four months. I have no idea where she is now. Long story. Anyway, Liz over there asked everything but my social security number. I told her we were dating as a distraction. She invited me to Easter dinner on your behalf, and I'm to make you go. Think you can pretend to be my girlfriend for a few hours?"

10

Mark walked down the alley that led to the off-campus housing. The college was surrounded by street after street of houses that had been cut up into cheap apartments for students. Exams would start after everyone got back from the long holiday weekend. and he was ready to get this graduation business over. He had an internship waiting for him at one of the biggest airplane manufacturing companies in the world. His engineering degree was only the beginning of a great career in aerodynamics and design. Or at least he hoped. He'd gone straight through to a doctorate degree and now needed some serious work experience on his résumé. He couldn't exactly list all his job skills.

Mark emerged from the alley next to his favorite

local burger and bar place that many students frequented. Cheap food and cheap beer. There was also other stuff available behind the bar, but only a few people were aware of the other substances for purchase.

Mark entered the scrappy-looking place and was greeted by his friend Roman, the bartender. "Burger with the works and loaded fries, yeah?"

"Already on the grill." He winked at Mark in secret code. "Need some special sauce with that burger?"

Mark grinned. "You know it, brother. S'been a long week."

The bartender smirked. "I hear ya. I got a new recipe this week. I think you're gonna like it."

"Hit me up."

The food arrived a few minutes later in a white bag with grease stains showing through the sides. Mark paid and took the bag to a scarred table that had been in this place longer than he'd been alive. Another guy sat nearby, busily scarfing down his own food. From the hoodie, shorts, and longboard, he was another student, probably in the graduate program by the looks of him. Mark gave him a nod and a peace sign before digging into his bag.

He unwrapped the foil-covered burger and took a

huge bite. Half the toppings slipped out the other side and plopped onto a napkin. Mark scooped it up and popped the mass into his mouth. The fries swam in a puddle of oil that gathered at the bottom of the cardboard container.

Roman double-boxed it, but not just for the grease runoff. There was something else between them that Mark was interested in: a small, thin baggie that contained a tiny paper. Mark discreetly looked around at the other patrons before pulling out the paper and placing it under his tongue. The sweet flavor surprised him. Normally, acid tasted bitter, but the bartender said it was a new recipe. He fished the paper around with his tongue until it dissolved.

The high started immediately, the room swimming out of focus. *Damn, that was fast,* Mark thought as the effects picked up. Purple clouds floated in the air, and the music over the speakers blurred into a cacophony of sound. His left arm tingled as it lost sensation. He looked down at his hand, which had fallen into his lap unresponsive. There was no movement when he commanded it. Soon the right one followed the same pattern.

He never considered himself a drug user, as he only partook when he needed to relax, like before exams. His tolerance wasn't particularly high, so the effects were usually intense, but this onslaught was on a whole other level. Too much. Too soon. Too hard.

Something's wrong. That thought came just before the pain hit. His lungs stopped working, and his heart cramped. His arms remained frozen. *Fuck me!* He tried to stand, but his legs gave out and he fell to the sticky floor. *Air! I need air!* He tried to call out, but his voice was nothing more than a squeak.

The bartender heard the crash and came over to investigate. "Shit, man, you okay?"

Mark only gasped as his throat closed and the blackness took over.

THE MAN IN THE HOODIE TUCKED HIS longboard under his arm and left quickly as the other patrons gathered around the choking student. No one noticed or stopped him as he went out to the sidewalk, dropped the flat piece of wood onto the ground, and mounted its surface. Three pumps of his long leg had him sailing down the smooth concrete away from the college spot. The people out and about on campus paid no mind at all to the common sight of a student on a skateboard between classes.

He arrived at the main student center and popped the board up with his toes before entering the building. Two girls were on their way out, and he held the door open for them, giving them a big smile and a nod.

One of the girls giggled. "Thanks. I haven't seen you around before."

He shrugged. "It's a big campus."

"There's a party over in the C dorms tonight. Wanna come?"

He smiled at her and fingered the scar by his left ear. "I have plans tonight, but maybe next time."

11

THE CLUB WAS AT FULL CAPACITY. YOU'D THINK a holy weekend like Easter would keep some people at home. Nope. The dancers and waitresses sported bunny ears and tails this Saturday night. Wolf wondered how many of them went to midnight mass before they came to work.

He stifled a yawn and shifted on the stool under him. This was his station, close to the stage to watch for any men getting a little too excited about tits and ass. The crowd seemed more riled up than normal tonight. Candie was up there working the pole and sliding her hands over her glistening body. Silvery glitter drifted to the stage floor. Wolf's only thought was the bitching from the cleaners when they had to deal with that stuff. He gave up trying to hide his fatigue and let his mouth stretch wide.

"Bored or tired?" Camshaft walked up with a hefty cup of coffee in his hand. "Here. Baghouse wanted some, so I made a pot."

"Thanks. Pulling double duty here and at the coffee shop is getting tough." He took a healthy swig of the dark brew. "I used to go all night and all day on just a few hours of sleep no problem. Not so much anymore."

"How much longer you think you'll be needed there?" Camshaft asked as he tilted back a bottle of Iron City Beer.

"Don't know. Madge comes in the afternoons to help bake for the next day, but Jazz and I are the ones who keep the doors open right now. Six to six every fucking day, and then she goes to do another job. I don't see how she does it."

"You're doing it too."

"Yeah, but I'm used to it." He drained the rest of the mug with a frown.

Cheers suddenly erupted, and Wolf didn't have to look up to figure out Candie's top was now off and her breasts out. He really didn't care.

Camshaft raised the bottle again. "The Slaggers are still buggin' the vape shop guy. He said they're makin' real threats now about burnin' him out if he doesn't play their way."

Wolf frowned. "As in setting the place on fire? It would spread to the other shops on that row. Bad idea."

"I'm thinkin' the Slaggers aren't known for their intelligence. If that store suddenly bursts into flame, I expect we'll already have the number one suspects in mind."

Wolf regarded his empty mug. The coffee was strong, but not as good as what Jazz made him. One corner of his mouth lifted as he recalled her expression when he asked her to be his pretend girlfriend. So fucking cute.

"We'll keep an eye out for trouble. Scrap will want us to keep it all in-house, so to speak." He sighed. "Not feeling this shit. I'd rather not go to war with the Slaggers, but we may have to if something goes down."

Camshaft shifted his feet and leaned back with his eyes on the stage. "I hope it doesn't come to that."

Wolf grunted, not needing to voice his agreement. War between the clubs was likely to go very bad quickly, and someone always got killed or at least hurt. Very often that someone was a civilian or bystander with no club affiliation. Wolf had seen enough blood and had no desire to go down that road if it could be avoided. His former career left a bad taste in his mouth, and he made himself get out before the darkness consumed him. Very few people knew about his past, and he preferred to keep it that way.

Another cheer from the crowd, and Wolf glanced to the stage to see Candie wearing nothing but a thin G-string and stilettos. How the hell she danced in those things was beyond him.

"You good to finish up tonight? I need to get some sleep. Big day tomorrow."

Camshaft drained his beer and set the empty bottle aside. "What? You going to mass or something?"

Wolf grinned. "Nah. I got a family dinner date."

12

Jazz breathed in and out several times as she faced the door to her parents' house. She wasn't prone to panic attacks, but being in the same room with both her mother and sister was enough to drive a saint to drink. Her father generally stayed out of the way and plodded along in his life as an observer, not a participator. Hopefully, Hugo would be here to help mediate any drama.

The houses in this neighborhood were built long and narrow, fitting so close together that there was little to no room to walk between them. A few of them had driveways, but most cars were parked on the street.

Jazz shifted from foot to foot on the unpainted

concrete steps that led to the entrance. She carried a sugar cake and a box of Danishes as her contribution.

Just a couple hours. That's all. Then you can go home and binge-watch Deep Space Nine *the rest of the night.*

The internal pep talk wasn't helping much.

Wolf told her he would meet her here, as he had something he needed to do before he came. She was still shocked as hell that he said he would be her pretend boyfriend for the day. *Boyfriend* didn't sound right for a man like Wolf, nor did the *pretend* part. It was more like a repeated movie trope from the Hallmark Channel. Men didn't do favors like this for random women in real life. Or was it her doing a favor for him? It didn't make a lot of sense for Wolf to come to Easter dinner to prove some-thing to Liz. He didn't know the woman, so why did it matter?

Jazz shook her head. Gah, she needed some serious Vulcan logic to figure out Wolf and his motive. Even so, it was a nice gesture, and she would consider this more like a friend helping a friend.

She glanced at her *Doctor Who* watch and noted it was five minutes after three. Technically, she was late, but Wolf wasn't here yet. Should she go in and see the sneer on her sister's face that the alleged boyfriend didn't show up or wait and listen to the inevitable lecture from her mom on punctuality?

Thankfully, Hugo ambled down the cracked sidewalk, his round face bursting into a big grin when he spotted her. "Yo, sis! Whassup?"

Jazz smiled back. "Yo, bro! I'm soooo glad you're here. I can't face the lion's den without backup." She hugged her brother, who only stood up to her shoulder.

"Whatcha got in the bag?" he asked in his lisping accent. His glasses made his brown eyes look huge.

"Treats from the bakery. Did you bring any from your work?"

His grin got bigger. "Duh. I make dog treats. Remember?" He used his most sarcastic tone but giggled at his own words.

"I don't think the kids can tell the difference."

Hugo burst out laughing and showed his short teeth with their slight underbite. "I can't give dog treats to Liz's kids. That's dumb." His face filled with delight. "Look at that!" He pointed excitedly at a spot in the distance. The rumble of the flame-covered motorcycle got louder as the rider pulled the machine up next to them.

Jazz froze. This was the perfect slo-mo movie scene, and she didn't want to miss a moment. In one motion, Wolf kicked down the stand and dismounted the bike, swinging one leg over the seat, stretching his jeans tight. He removed his helmet and shook out his hair, letting the curling length fly and settle around his face. Those green-gold orbs of his blinked slowly as their gazes met, and her ovaries started singing the *Hallelujah* chorus. She closed her eyes and counted to ten, then did it again. She opened them to see Wolf and Hugo fist-bump in greeting.

"Cool motorcycle. Are you dating my sister?" Hugo chortled as he turned to face Jazz. "Liz told me you have a boyfriend now. I came to meet him. I wanted to see for myself who would be brave enough to date my favorite sister."

"You think she shouldn't be with me?" Wolf asked with amusement dancing in his eyes.

"No way. *You* shouldn't be with *her.* Run away while you can. I'll cover for ya."

Wolf threw back his head and laughed long and loud. "Hugo, my brother, you are cool as hell." He slung an arm around the shorter man. "Let's go eat. You coming, baby?"

Ooooo, he called me baby again!

Jazz shook her head to get her thoughts in order and to quell the butterflies in her stomach. "Okay, then. Dibs on when Mom brings up mass. I say before the meat is served."

"YOU CAN'T GET A GOOD PORK ROAST AROUND here anymore. I went to three different grocers and the butcher shop over on Fifth. Terrible service."

Jazz cringed as her mother, Delores Hickling, started the expected rant. Just after the woman's ample backside hit the chair, she asked the dreaded question. "Yinz go to mass this morning, yeah?" It was directed at the entire table, but Jazz felt the weight of that stare on herself. She exchanged a look with her brother, who tried not to choke on his suppressed laughter.

Wolf answered with a surprising yes. "Early sunrise service." He picked up the bowl of mashed potatoes to serve himself and plopped a spoonful onto Jazz's plate before handing it off to her dad.

The dining alcove was small and crowded with six adults sitting around the table. The two older kids were in the kitchen at a card table, making more of a mess than eating. The baby sat in a high chair between his mom and his grandfather. Liz and Hugo were across from Wolf and Jazz. Her parents were stationed at the head and foot of the table. Jazz noted that these were the same places everyone had occupied for decades. The only exception was Wolf.

Liz had gone all out, with full-blown makeup and hair. Three pregnancies had left her with humongous breasts, and Jazz was sure there was a major push-up bra under those puppies. The top halves were exposed and moved around like Jell-O. Jazz wondered if Wolf would be impressed or disinterested. The man got to see naked women nightly at the strip club he worked for, so a set of ample ta-tas shouldn't hold more than a passing interest to him, right?

Liz batted her eyes as she picked up a dish and handed it across to Wolf. "I bought an apple pie from Phyliss's store yesterday. I hope it's good this time. The last one I got was too sweet. She was out of Graeter's, so I had to get Breyer's ice cream for the top."

Delores screwed up her face in revulsion. "That's not gonna taste right. Didja at least get the cheese for your father?"

Liz rolled her eyes and dropped the charming facade for a moment. "Yeah, I did. It's revolting, though. Who else but him eats a slice of sharp cheddar on their apple pie?"

Jazz held back her "I do," but she heard it anyway. All eyes centered on Wolf, who had spoken.

Hugo blinked behind his glasses. "You do that too? I thought Dad and Jazz were the only weirdos."

Jazz turned red at her brother's comment. "Hugo!"

Wolf wasn't fazed. "It's actually pretty common, especially among people of English descent. My mom always served it that way."

Delores raised her eyebrows. "She lives here in Pittsburgh?"

He shook his head as he raised a forkful of green beans. "No. She died some years ago and is buried up in Maine, where she was from. My father died about a year after she did."

"I'm sorry for your loss," Jazz whispered lightly.

Wolf looked at her warmly. "It was a long time ago, but thanks, babe."

Babe, baby, gah! Jazz's insides melted every time she heard an endearment from him. *It's not going to last. It's only for today.*

"I think it's gross," Ian yelled from the kitchen.

Jazz's liquid heat froze instantly. "Quit being rude. It's okay for people to like different things."

Wolf let out a huge laugh. "Don't worry about it, Jazz. The kid is entitled to his opinions."

Liz, however, took her opportunity. "Can't get much different than Jazzy. Always has her head in the clouds or on the computer. Right, Mom?"

Delores picked up the familiar topic and expanded as she assumed a dramatic air. "Oh my gawd, all those science fiction space books she read as a kid. If I heard another word about Martians or spaceships that talk, I'd lose my mind. She's always dreamin' of some weird fantasy world and makin' up stories. She even tried to build a rocket thing so she could send messages to all the aliens. All she did was make a big mess and nearly burned the house down when she tried to light it. Got that idea from a book, I bet."

Jazz closed her eyes as one of her childhood's most embarrassing moments was revealed in front of Wolf. That was a major sore spot between her and her mother, as the woman constantly brought them up to company and whoever would listen. She hoped it would stop there, but Liz, in her true form, added to the mix.

"Yeah, I remember her begging for a library card so she got all her books for free. Stacks of them. You'd think with all that reading she did in college, she'd be doing something big like NASA or something instead of playing on her computer and pouring coffee."

Delores heaved a martyred sigh. "Four years wasted. All that money she borrowed. It's a shame. Thank gawd we didn't pay for any of that. No, after my kids turned eighteen, they were on their own."

Jazz cleared her throat. This was another sore spot. It didn't matter that she paid off those school loans within four years instead of twenty. That success would never be acknowledged. Neither of her siblings went to college, let alone graduated with honors. Hugo found his place in the world and moved out a year ago to his group home. He loved his job and was good at it. Their mom hated it, but she couldn't stop him. Liz moved in and out with regularity and had never had a job that paid enough to support her or her kids. Jazz was the only one of the three who truly stood on her own two feet. But that never seemed to matter, as her mother and sister apparently had this constant need to put her down. Soon her hair would be brought up, then her state of singlehood, then her age and her clothes, then—

"Libraries are one of the coolest places for a kid. I used to hang there all the time." Wolf's deep voice held a note of admonishment and matter-of-factness. "I liked early sci-fi myself. Jules Verne is a classic. H.G. Wells is another. My favorites are Ray Bradbury, Isaac Asimov, and Frank Herbert."

Jazz's eyes popped open and darted to the man sitting next to her. He put food in his mouth, chewed, and swallowed at a slow and steady pace. Hugo also kept his head down and continued eating. His way of dealing with Delores and Liz was to ignore them or pretend he didn't understand them until they ran out of steam. Then he'd leave and go back to his room in the community home he'd chosen. Some people with Down's were nonverbal and had a lot of comprehension trouble, but Hugo understood more than people gave him credit for. Jazz noticed the smirk on his face.

Wolf took a sip from his water glass and set it back done. "I'm guessing the first book your mom mentioned is *The Martian Chronicles*. What's the other one?"

"*The Ship Who Sang* by Anne McCaffrey."

"I'm not familiar with that one. You'll have to tell me about it sometime." He kept eating and talking between bites. "As far as college, I don't think education in any form is a waste. I never got to finish my degree, but I still value my time at the university."

Wolf went to college? Why didn't I know that? "What did you study?"

"I debated between mechanical engineering and biomedical engineering." He smiled and met Jazz's wide eyes. "I wanted to design and build surgical robots before I went into the military."

Hugo couldn't stand it anymore. He let out a whooping laugh and pointed at his sister. "Did you hear that, Jazz? He's a big nerd just like you!"

"That's... that's amazing and really cool. Why did you stop going to school?"

His expression darkened a bit, but the smile stayed on his face. "Another time, babe."

Delores huffed. "Robots, libraries, books, whatever. It's all a bunch of hooey unless it puts money in the bank. College? Useless in my opinion."

Wolf eyed the woman but kept his mouth shut. Jazz flushed with embarrassment and tried to think of something to distract the table. She was fully aware of the disdain her family had for her hobbies and education in general. It was surprising and kinda cool to hear that Wolf was into sci-fi too.

Liz stepped into the fray and picked up the basket of rolls to hand to Wolf. "So, do you have brothers and sisters?"

Wolf took the bread and carefully pulled it open. "No siblings. A few cousins up in Maine, but we're not close. Pass the butter, would ya, Hugo?"

Her brother grinned nonstop as he handed the rectangular dish to the biker. Jazz watched him cut and spread the yellow pat. She noted the sprinkles of dark hair on the backs of his hands.

She discreetly checked her phone for the time. Roughly thirty minutes in so far. Her plan was to make it to the hour, then leave. She was so focused on how soon she could escape that she almost missed Wolf's question.

"Anyone have a favorite sci-fi movie of all time?"

Liz rolled her eyes and flopped back in her chair. "Oh my gawd, please not the movies. She's bad enough about the books."

Hugo frowned. "Movies are cool. You're just too stupid to like them."

Liz turned red underneath her makeup. "Mom! You gonna let him speak to me like that?"

"Christ on a cracker, I just wanted one day of peace with my family, and this is what I get!" Delores snapped.

Jazz covered her flaming face with her hands and leaned over to Wolf as she took the butter dish from him. *Thanks for the butter. They're always like this. I love movies.* "They're love butter." *God, please take me now!*

This time it was Wolf who burst out laughing. "What I wouldn't give to go inside that head of yours for a few minutes to see how it works. One of my favorite things about you. That and your hair."

Jazz blushed for the umpteenth time, but in her head, she preened. "Thanks. I like your hair too."

Hugo grinned. "Me too. How did you get the gray part?"

"My grandmother. She had this shock of gray hair all her life. People used to ask her where she got it done, and she'd always answer, 'Genetics.' She was a Mainer through and through. I remember when she took me to the shore. The beach was full of rounded smooth rocks and pebbles instead of white sand. Not many people."

Hugo blinked. "That's weird. A beach with no sand?"

Wolf wiped his mouth with his napkin and placed it over his clean plate. "I'm not kidding. I'll take you and your sister there someday to see it."

Jazz wanted to groan. "You shouldn't tell him that unless you mean it."

Wolf turned to face her, and her heart fluttered at his direct gaze. "I don't say things I don't mean, babe. Ever."

Hugo whooped loud and long. He raised both fisted hands in the air. "Woo-hoo! I'm going to Maine! I'm going to Maine! Road trip!"

THE REST OF THE SUNDAY MEAL WAS NO different. Little barbed remarks came from Liz and Delores to the point that Wolf found it hard to believe Jazz shared DNA with the two women. The kids finished eating—or rather making a mess—and started running around the house, smacking into things and generally going crazy.

Hugo finished his food and kept quiet. Wolf had no doubts that some people would look at his features and make assumptions, but for all the young man's challenges, he was brilliant.

Hugo faked a huge yawn at the table. "I'm so full. I need to go home and take a long nap. I got work tomorrow early."

Delores scoffed. "I don't understand why you had to move to that place when you have a perfectly good home right here."

Wolf noticed Hugo's eye twitch once and guessed this was the reason he moved out in the first place.

"I gotta grow up someday, Mom. Besides, I like baking dog treats. I'm in charge of a whole crew now." His grin was infectious, and Wolf raised his hand across the table for a fist bump.

"Way to go, brother."

Hugo giggled and addressed Jazz. "Did you hear that, sis? He called me brother."

Jazz helped clear the dessert dishes while Delores complained about the dishwasher not working very well and the off-brand tabs she bought because Cascade was so expensive. "I'll have to rewash everything by hand anyways."

Wolf swore under his breath. Was there anything in this world that woman wouldn't nitpick?

He was finally able to take his leave when Hugo gave another fake yawn and declared he had to go home. "Jazz, come out with me a minute?" Hugo asked.

"Sure."

Once they were outside, Hugo gave his sister a big hug before ambling down the street.

Wolf looked at the departing man. "How far does he have to go?"

"He'll grab the bus one block over and take it back to the home. It's about a twenty-minute trip."

"He's good using the bus?"

Jazz's voice got tight. "Hugo has trouble with some things, but getting himself on and off the bus is not one of them. He has his route and routines, which keep him on track as long as no one disturbs them. He needs reminders from time to time, but he's perfectly capable of caring for himself."

"I didn't mean to imply anything. I have an extra helmet with me and thought he'd like a ride home."

"Oh." Her contrite face almost made him laugh.

"How 'bout you? Do you want a ride home?" He waited to see if she would utter one of her ridiculous phrases.

She glanced over at the front of her parents' house. "Um… I'd like that, but I have my own bike with me."

Wolf looked down at her, but his attention was on the two women with their heads together in the window, chattering away. From Jazz's nervousness, no doubt it was about the two of them and how they could possibly be together.

It pissed him off.

He didn't know her that well, but everything he'd learned about the woman, he liked. Her dedication to helping Madge and Bill stood at the forefront, but each time he peeled back a layer, he found something else. Her talent for computer programming and her hacking skills and willingness to take on the scammers was impressive. She rode a bicycle and made a killer cup of coffee. The *Star Trek* paraphernalia in her house should have given him a clue about her love for science fiction, but finding out the bit about the library and book preferences was more icing on the cake.

He picked up a piece of blue hair that hung over her shoulder. "They're watching us right now."

Jazz gave a nervous huffing laugh. "I know, and I'm not surprised. They need something else to talk about. All the usual topics are getting stale."

His fingers traced her jawline, and he saw her go rigid. "You gonna hit me if I give them something new?"

"Like what?"

He answered by lowering his head, taking her mouth, and swallowing the tiny squeak she uttered. He took the opportunity to run the tip of his tongue over the seam of her lips, and to his delight, she opened for him. Without a second's hesitation, he dove in. Coffee, cinnamon, and sugar—his favorite flavors. Teasing Jazz had become one of his preferred pastimes, but he hadn't counted on the way he reacted. His own body flushed with heat, and his dick jumped to attention.

She must have sensed it, as her body locked in place. Fight-or-flight took over, and Wolf figured flight would win. He kept his hand just under her cheek to hold her in place as he ended the kiss. "That should top those two off for a while, yeah?"

"Mm-hmm."

"Thanks for the invite. I had a great time."

"Mm-hmm."

"I'll see you tomorrow."

"M'kay."

He stifled a laugh as he turned and walked away, but he couldn't help glancing over his shoulder to see Jazz rapidly fanning herself with both hands.

Yes, he was enjoying this way too much.

13

Henry Blaylock punched his code into the time clock after clearing his desk in the cubicle he was assigned to. He was a small but important cog in the wheels of the giant international shipping company. Most of his coworkers thought of him as nothing more than a computer geek and paper pusher, but keeping up with the manifests and inventory was a critical part of the whole machine. Without him, the network crash from a few weeks ago would have been disastrous. It was only his acuity and obsessive attention to detail that kept the work flowing.

Henry smiled at his wayward thoughts. If only they knew.

He pushed his thick glasses up on his nose as he

walked to his car. The day shift was on their way out, and the night shift was entering. Henry frowned as he spotted the woman who took his place at the shared office space. When he returned to work tomorrow morning, there would be candy wrappers, a dirty coffee cup, and skewed paper stacks at his meticulously kept desk. He'd complained about the mess before, but the woman never paid attention. Henry swore she left the desk in shambles now just to irritate him further.

He drove to his condo, careful to obey all the traffic laws. A few horns blared at him when he paused too long at stop signs, but he never exceeded the 20-kph limit for his neighborhood.

"Rules are rules," he muttered as he pulled loose the bow tie at his throat. He swept a hand over his thinning sand-colored hair and resisted the urge to give the driver behind him the finger. A friend of his had done that and earned a road-rage beating. Henry was not a big man, barely topping sixty-three kilograms. Any fight he ever engaged in would see him on the losing side.

He pulled into the lot and parked with precision in his spot, backing up twice until the car was perfectly centered and straight. He'd moved to this condo high-rise specifically for the clean lawns and weed-free mulch. Ottawa was an expensive place to live, but he could afford the luxury. His unit was on the top floor and overlooked a large pond. The only eyesore was the shipping yard on the other side, but he really shouldn't complain about that. After all, they were his employers.

As he reached his front door, the woman who lived in the condo across from him came out with her yappy little Pomeranian on a leash. Henry's nose wrinkled at her disheveled appearance and the amount of dog hair on her clothes. The animal growled and barked at him, and he backed away from the dirty creature.

"I'm sorry," the woman muttered and picked up the snapping dog. "He's just being protective."

Henry's lip curled. "You should always keep him leashed and muzzled. If he bites anyone, you'll have to move. Rules are rules after all, eh?"

She gave him a nasty look and walked to the elevator.

Henry ignored them as he entered his home, traded his shoes for slippers, and placed the black loafers in a cupboard beside the door. The walls were light gray and uniform throughout the place with a darker gray carpet to blend. His furniture was black-and-white, including his bedroom. No pictures hung on the walls, no knickknacks or decorations anywhere, and nothing sat on the gray granite kitchen countertops. The coffee maker and every other small appliance were stored away in the cabinets to keep all surfaces clutter free. Henry liked his place to be squeaky clean. He hated cooking because of potential splatters on the sparkling stovetop and relied heavily on prepackaged meals he could heat and throw the wrappers away after.

He pulled an instant dinner from the stack of boxes in his freezer and put it in the microwave, exactly in the center of the spinning plate. Seven minutes later, he took the hot meal out and placed it on a tray along with cutlery and a folded napkin. He had no dining room table and didn't entertain in his home. Guests were messy, and he didn't want that in his living space.

Instead, the dining area held his home computer setup. Multiple screens surrounded him on either side of the bay window, with several towers and other components that were kept neatly stacked in their places. He opened the curtains to let the light in but kept the window closed to keep any bugs out. A small table sat next to him, which he placed his food tray on before powering up his elaborate electronics.

As the machines whirred to life, he raised his eyes

to the window and spotted his neighbor walking around the pond with her annoying dog. Again, his lip curled at the prancing mutt. He hoped she was smart enough to pick up any shit it left on the ground. The smell was revolting, and he could almost sense the odor from where he sat. Disgusting.

He turned to his food and cut it into uniform pieces, chewing each mouthful ten times before swallowing. In five minutes or less, he was done eating and tossed the paper container into the lidded trash can next to his massive desk.

He had just opened his browser when a dizzy spell hit him. He was surprised to find himself sweating and gasping for air. The pungent odor was real and not the imagined dog shit from his neighbor. He wondered if she'd brought him a canine present and left it outside his door, and that was where the nasty smell came from. He got up and discovered his legs didn't work right. His head bounced off the floor as he met the carpet with a thud. The muscles in his legs spasmed, and he gasped again, this time heaving as his lungs rebelled. Everything he'd just put in his stomach came back up to coat the carpet in vomit. He wiped a hand over his mouth and it came away bloody, leaving a big red smear on the light gray.

I'm coughing blood? His heart pounded as if it was ready to burst through his chest.

His last thought was how that would leave a stain.

ONE FLOOR UP, THE MAINTENANCE MAN WAS finishing a job in that condo unit. The woman who owned it was an artist, and she kept her windows open all the time because of the strong paint fumes. The carpets were toast, but it was her plumbing that was the problem. The paint and other stuff she put down the drains caused the pipes to rot out and be a problem. He'd replaced a number of them, some with ABS, others with copper.

The woman watched him with barely concealed impatience. "Are you almost done? I don't want to lose more of the light than I have to, eh?"

The man scratched a heavy gray-bearded jowl and hiked up his work pants. "I'll be done soon."

He grunted as he pushed his bulk under the kitchen sink to test the connections. "I'll check the bathroom one more time, and then I should be done, eh?"

The artist sighed dramatically. "You've been here for hours already."

"'Tis a big job, miss."

She huffed again and crossed her arms. "I hate this. I have all this creative energy flowing, and I can't get to my stuff with all those tanks over there." She gestured to the row of cylinders of different gases to help him with the soldering. They were lined up in the main room near the open window like soldiers ready for battle.

"Just leave them alone, and I'll take care of them soon."

Another huff came from her painted mouth, and she started tapping her bare toes on the carpet with impatience. The sound was muffled, but it irritated the maintenance man anyway. He took his time, checking the seals, testing the pressure, and cleaning up the newly soldered joints of the pipes. Finally he was finished.

"Okay, ma'am, you can have your space back."

She sneered a little. The man's overgrown facial hair needed some serious trimming. "Whatever. I'm getting my stuff from the other room."

The maintenance man put away his tools in their precise places, then turned to deal with the four gas tanks. He glanced over his shoulder toward the room the artist disappeared into and sent up a prayer that she would stay away from him for the next few minutes. He checked the regulators to see that all four tanks were empty before shutting off the valves. Then he pulled up the carpet right at the edge and revealed four holes drilled into the ceiling leading to the apartment below. Four small hoses connected to the tanks and concentrated the nitrogen dioxide that flowed into the space underneath, making the air toxic to breathe. He might have overdone it a little, but the gas would dissipate now, rendering it undetectable, and the cause of death undetermined.

The man pulled the hoses out and plugged the holes, disguising them thoroughly so they couldn't be found.

"Are you done?" The screech came from the back room and grated on his ears. If there was any leeway in this assignment, there would be a second body in this building tonight.

"Yes, ma'am." He loaded the tanks onto a rolling cart and stood with a slight bend in his back, letting his puffed-out gut hang over his pants. "Oh, the older I get, the more I want to retire."

The artist strolled back into the main living area and examined her fingernails. The worker's inflection was odd, but she really didn't care. "Please just don't talk and finish soon, okay?"

He smiled, showing stained teeth, and she cringed

as a sudden frisson of fear traveled her spine. He reached up and scratched at a scar just in front of his left ear. "I'm done. Have a nice day."

Ten minutes later, all four tanks and his toolboxes were secured in the wagon, and the man was wheeling them away. The artist closed the door and wrinkled her nose at the sour scent that followed him.

Bathing should be a requirement, she thought as she readied her paints and opened her windows wider to air out her apartment.

14

"Yes, ma'am, you will have to go to the CVS and get four gift cards in the amount of one thousand dollars each. You must pay this fine, or the IRS will come to arrest you."

Jazz rolled her eyes before answering. "The CVS is all the way on the other side of town. Cain't I just go to my bank? It's a lot closer for me to walk. Uphill. Both ways."

Today, her voice modulator was set to her favorite old lady voice speaking with a thick Southern accent.

"No, you can't go to your bank. This is the SSN, ma'am. Please do as I say and go to the CVS. The police are on their way right now."

Jazz continued to type. "My knees have been givin' me so much trouble lately."

"I'm sorry to hear that, but we need to get this debt paid or else you will go to jail."

"I'll call my grandson to come get me."

"No, ma'am, you must go yourself. Don't tell anyone what you're doing."

Ha. Gotcha. "Give up, Sparky. Check your screen."

Jazz didn't bother to hear the shocked dismay of the scammer as she erased not only his computer but crippled his entire operating system. It had been quite some time since she'd taken anyone down, and tonight she'd gotten several of them in a row. Nothing like the big one she did a month or so ago. She'd been staying away from the bigger call centers, but it was still satisfying to stop whoever she could from harming anyone else.

She leaned back in her desk chair and ran her hands over her tired face. Between the bakery and the database job, she pulled roughly seventy-odd working hours per week, and it was starting to show. Wolf came to the bakery in the mornings and worked with her when possible. He did the register and treats until Madge came to take over for a few hours. Then he visited Bill in the afternoons, napping there until he had to go to work at Attic. Her schedule was similar. She slept when she had a chance, but the catnaps she usually took weren't enough anymore, and fatigue was catching up with her. Not once during their many hours together had he brought up the kiss he gave her in front of her parents' house.

Nor had he repeated it.

Of course she'd also become completely self-conscious and tongue-tied around him. Would she appear flirty if she talked to him or desperate? Or pathetic? Did he like her or just find her amusing? The pretend boyfriend/girlfriend thing was a cute little trope for a cheap romance movie, but in real life, that sort of thing didn't really happen, right?

She sighed as she stretched her arms over her head and several bones cracked in her neck and spine. How much longer could she keep up this schedule? Something had to give, and soon.

A message popped up on her screen.

Copperpot100: You hear from Bomber123? He's been dark for a while.

Jazzyhands: No, I haven't.

Copperpot100: He's always online between 8:00 p.m. and midnight every night like clockwork for years. He hasn't been on in a week.

Jazzyhands: Maybe he's on vay-cay?

Copperpot100: He doesn't take vacations.

That was true. Bomber123 was so regular in his hours, it was almost like punching a time card into a job.

Jazzyhands: Maybe he's sick?

Copperpot100: Glynda has been out for a while too.

Jazzyhands: I'm not sure what you're trying to say.

The bouncing dots stayed still for a brief moment, then starting moving.

Copperpot100: There's been some movement on the dark web about revenge against those who took down that huge network a while back. Scumbags will talk a big game when they're only voices over the phone or emails over the internet. That shakedown took out a major network and then some. They're still recovering from it on the legit side as well as the call centers. We're talking a shit ton of lost revenue. A few hundred bucks, no one blinks an eye. A few thousand will raise an eyebrow. A few hundred thousand, someone's pissed. We're talking millions right now.

Jazz read the message twice. It was true she always felt safe sitting anonymously behind the screen, moving a cursor and clicking the mouse. No names. No locations. No cybertrails. Not one shred of an ID of any kind. All the shielders knew about one another were their screennames. Jazz took care to erase and scrub her activities, deleting any information from the web that might come back on her. The thought that someone had found a way to identify any of their group was frightening.

Jazzyhands: You think something has happened to them? Like physically? I hope you're joking with me. We're so careful all the time to leave no traces.

Copperpot100: You are. I am. I don't know that the rest of the shielders are always consistent. Glynda has a bunch of handles, like CatLady50 she uses on Tinder. Check with me from time to time if you notice someone messing in your network. I'm getting a bad vibe about this. Best-case is I'm suspicious as shit. Worst-case is I'm right and we need to lie low for a while. Keep off the grid until I contact you. Got it?

Jazz folded her hands together for a moment. Perhaps Glynda and Bomber were both just out at the same time. It could happen. There were other active shielders out there still, right? No reason to get all freaked out.

Still, there was that old saying that just because you're paranoid doesn't mean they aren't out to get you.

Jazzyhands: Okay. Stay sharp, Copperpot. I'm down for the night.

At least that was her plan until she got a text.

A few minutes later, she was dressed and out the door.

15

Wolf eyed the man at the far end of the stage. The dude had been here dozens of times and always requested Candie for a lap dance on Thursday nights. The club had four private rooms for that purpose. The doors had small windows that were not allowed to be blocked, nor the door itself locked. Generally, the dancers got to decide if any touching was allowed, but for the most part, the men who paid them for the private dances kept their hands to themselves. Wolf thought it was worrisome to see him here again on a Saturday night, but maybe the dude had extra money or just had a bad week.

Wolf could relate. Part of his bad mood might be the frustrating crap between him and Jazz. After the Easter dinner and surprising kiss, she'd changed her behavior toward him, and he hated it. When they were at the bakery, she spoke only when she had to and went out of her way to avoid him. Her mixed words and phrases he found so cute had all but dried up. Every single time he made an attempt to banter or tease her, she clammed up tight. He asked her what was wrong, and the only answer he got was "Nothing" or "Nothing, I'm fine."

It was driving him bananas, and frankly, he missed their interaction.

The kiss surprised him. When he talked her into that pretend thing for her parents, he did it partially out of amusement and partially out of curiosity. The woman intrigued him, and he found himself wanting to know more and more about her. He genuinely enjoyed her company, something he couldn't say about other women he'd known. The interactions with her family showed him another side of her he hadn't expected—vulnerability.

It pissed him off to hear her mom and sister putting her down for what he considered her successes, and the kiss was supposed to be a way to mess with them.

Instead, it set off a bomb inside him, and he wanted more.

A lot more.

It frustrated him that Jazz was stonewalling him, and every minute he was around her now, he spent an enormous amount of brainpower trying to figure out how to scale that fortress.

Candie approached the man at the bar and draped her arms over his shoulders. Wolf's focus changed, thinking the gesture was a bit too familiar. He flicked two fingers at Camshaft. "Who's the jagoff with Candie?"

"New boyfriend. He used to pay extra to touch her tits. She said he was a regular who politely came in a handkerchief before she finished a lap dance, always thanked her, and left a generous tip. She developed a soft spot for him and started 'dating' him." Cam put the word *dating* in air quotes. "I don't know how that works when he still has to pay for it."

Tonight, the guy was drinking heavily and getting sloppy.

Wolf jutted his chin in the man's direction. "Keep an eye on him, yeah? Something's off."

There was a strange vibe in the air tonight. A tension he couldn't put his finger on, but he felt antsy, as if waiting for disaster to strike. He hoped it was just his own personal anxieties from the week at the bakery and this new thing with Jazz. Hopefully, whatever friction bothered him would pass into an easy Sunday. He was due for a day off.

"Candie is takin' her guy in the back for a private show. Room two," Camshaft shouted over the pounding music. Ellie was up on the stage in white star pasties, thigh-high lace stockings, and long fringe across her crotch.

"He paying for a lap dance or something else?"

Cam shook his head. "I don't know, man. It's a weird night."

So, Cam was sensing it too. Fuck. "Keep an eye on them, yeah?"

Ellie finished her dance and made the rounds for her tips. Men stuffed cash in her thong as she squatted and shook her bare ass in their faces. One reached for a pasty, and she deftly moved out of the way as she giggled and shook her finger at him in a naughty-boy gesture. Nadja was up next, but before she brandished her signature Dom whip routine, there was a major commotion at the front.

"Get out of my fuckin' way, asshole! I know that piece of shit is here!"

Fuck no. Wolf spotted the woman shoving and slapping at Camshaft, and his stomach flipped over. *What the hell is Liz doing here?*

He fired off a text to Jazz and pushed through the

crowd, not caring if he knocked a few of them over as he hurried to get to the fighting woman. She clawed at Cam's face and broke free.

"Let go of me, fuckwad. I wanna know where my gawddamn husband is hiding. Where the fuck is he?"

Wolf spoke in the commanding voice he used to have for new recruits. "What the fuck, Liz?"

"Wolf?" She stopped her tirade for a brief moment, looking up at him in surprise. "What the hell are you doing here? Does Jazzy know you go to titty bars?" Then her face twisted into absolute rage. "Ya know, I don't fuckin' care. You can take your sorry ass and go piss up a fuckin' rope. Where the fuck is Leo?"

Wolf blocked her way as she pushed and fought him. "I don't know who you're talking about. You need to calm the fuck down and go outside."

That set her off like a nuclear bomb. "Calm down? Kiss my fuckin' ass! Fuck you and your fuckin'... fuckin'...," she spluttered, out of words.

Wolf took the opportunity to herd her toward the door. "Outside, Liz."

"No!"

Wolf clamped down on his temper and ground his teeth. Obviously, she was worked up enough that reasoning was not going to cut it. He could simply bear-hug the woman and bodily carry her from the place, but how would Jazz feel about him manhandling her sister? The entirety of the club was focused on the drama there at the front, and it wouldn't be long before Scrap came down from his throne and tossed Liz out on her ass. Literally. The man didn't give a shit if it was a woman making trouble. He was an equal opportunity asshole to everyone.

Liz screeched again. "Leo! You son of a bitch, I know you're here!"

Fuck it, Wolf thought as he wrapped his arms around the woman and lifted her off her feet. One of her flailing legs caught his shin, and he grunted in pain. "Stop fighting me and this will go a lot easier."

She cussed him out as he hauled the struggling woman outside. She made contact twice more before he made it to the street. Camshaft blocked the entrance, and Wolf set Liz on her feet. She shoved at him, trying to get back into the building. "Get the fuck outta my way! I'm going in there!"

"No, you're not." He blocked her over and over when she tried to linebacker her way past him. Minutes passed, and Wolf had to admit the woman's stamina was impressive. She was not going to give up without a fight, and one of them would have to back down eventually. He hoped it wouldn't be him.

"What's going on?"

Oh thank God, Wolf thought as Jazz arrived. "Your sister's not happy. Says her husband, some guy named Leo, is in the club. She was out of control in there, and I had to make her leave."

"Leo is in there right now!" Liz yelled. Her red face was contorted with anger as she pointed at the club entrance.

"Liz, calm down," Jazz started, but then she was cut off much like Wolf had been.

"Don't you tell me what to do! My husband is here cheating on me with some stripper!"

"I thought you two were separated. Weren't you talking about some guy you met at the grocers?"

Liz ignored that sentence. "He's still my husband, dammit!"

Wolf blocked another rushing-the-door attempt. "Look, you can't go in there and make a scene. What does he look like?"

Liz huffed and jerked her phone impatiently from her pocket. She scrolled through the pictures until she found what she wanted and thrust the screen into Wolf's face. "Here he is. Leo the lyin' asshole."

Shit. Wolf glanced back at Camshaft and held up two fingers. His jaw tightened even more, and he wondered if his teeth would crack under the pressure. His friend raised his eyebrows and pursed his lips in a silent whistle. This was not going to be good.

"You know where he is, don't you?" Liz accused. Her hair was a ratty tangle from the fight to get her out of the club and her wild charges to get back in.

Jazz tried again. "There's a coffee shop not far away. Why don't we go there and wait while Wolf and his friend go look for Leo?"

"Fuck that! I'm not movin' until that jagoff comes out!"

"Come on, Liz, be reasonable."

"Fuck reasonable, and fuck you!" She punctuated the sentence by throwing her phone at Jazz, striking her on the cheek. Jazz yelped and jerked to the side from the impact. Camshaft swore and moved to block the out-of-control woman from any more physical shit.

Wolf lost his temper. "Oh hell no. That's not happening here. You have about a minute and a half before I call the police."

"I said I'm not leaving!'

"Suit yourself." He dialed 911 to make the report.

"Please, Liz. If you get arrested, who's gonna watch the boys tonight?" Jazz held her hand to her cheek but kept her distance.

"Mom 'n' Dad are at the house." She turned to

Wolf with an ugly sneer on her face. "Sure. Call the police. I'll report how you assaulted me."

Wolf rolled his eyes and kept his attention on the angry woman. Camshaft kept himself in front of her, arms out wide to keep her from running back into the club. No one could say he touched her, but he made sure she didn't come near the entrance or Wolf and Jazz.

Wolf made a come-here gesture to Jazz. "Let me see." He examined the spot with gentle fingers. There was a nice bruise forming but no blood. He wasn't sure he could hold back if she'd been cut.

Blue lights appeared but no sirens. This wasn't the first time the police had been called to the club, and Wolf was sure it wouldn't be the last, but since no guns were involved, he requested that they not come in hot.

"Yo, Wolf. What's up?" The officer approached casually. "Someone get a little too excited around the girls?"

"Not this time, Denny. Ex-wife showed up."

"We're just separated!" Liz's face was beet red, and she showed no signs of de-escalating.

Jazz stayed to the side, as if she realized there was nothing she could do but let the scene play out.

Wolf hated doing this, but Liz was not giving him any other choice. "That's her if you didn't catch it."

Officer Denny turned to Liz and started talking with a placating tone. Liz wasn't having it, and the words that came out of her mouth would make a sailor raise an eyebrow.

Jazz pulled at Wolf's arm to get his attention, still holding her cheek. "What's going to happen to her? Is she going to jail?"

Wolf sighed. "That's up to her and what she does next. Hey, Cam. Go get me some ice, yeah?"

Cam leaned in and kept his voice low. "I took a look at room two. He's… um… engaged with Candie."

Can there be any more shit to pile on tonight? Wolf's temper was about to explode. "You're fucking with me, right? Candie damn well knows there's no 'engagement' at the club. What the fuck are they doing?"

Camshaft's eyes shifted to the screaming woman and then to a curious Jazz. "They're busy. Uh, house special."

"We don't have house specials. Busy how?"

The younger man hesitated a moment more and finally said in a low voice, "She's giving him a blow job, and under the circumstances, I decided to let them finish instead of making more trouble."

"Fuck." Wolf raised his eyes to the dark sky and counted to ten. Then did it again. Not helping.

Jazz kept her silence. This was good, as another unholy screech erupted from Liz's mouth.

"You cocksucking fuckwad!"

Denny had his cuffs out and moved to put them on Liz. She, of course, screamed and fought back, making that task impossible without more force. Jazz stood to the side, her face incredulous, as if she couldn't believe the drama unfolding in front of her eyes.

As if that wasn't bad enough, the person who started all this mess appeared a second later.

"Liz? What the fuck are you doin' here? Hey, leggo my wife!"

"Fuck," Wolf repeated. *What else could go wrong?*

He regretted that thought a moment later when an old dark gray Buick drove by and opened fire.

16

THE BREATH RUSHED OUT OF JAZZ AS SHE HIT the ground. It took her a few moments to realize Wolf had tackled her and rolled to place her body underneath his. The deafening *rat-tat-tat-tat* of automatic rifles made her heart skip a few beats.

"Stay down," he ordered in a harsh growl.

Jazz didn't move. Her ears rang from the gunfire, and she barely made out the muffled sound of shouts and screeching tires.

"Fuck!" Wolf barked before shouting to the other people around them. "Cam, report!"

"I'm good. Got the sister with me. She's okay."

"Denny?"

"Check." The gravelly voice sounded like it floated

up from a deep well. "What kind of shit show have the Knights gotten into?"

"Club war. Slaggers MC."

Denny tsked as he got off the ground where he crouched. "You're kidding me. The Slaggers aren't a club. That one is an out-and-out gang."

Wolf grunted. "Tell me something I don't know."

Jazz cleared her throat. "Um… this is fun, but I'd really like to breathe now."

Wolf's eyes came down to hers, and he lifted himself off her just enough to take his own weight. "Did you get hit?"

Jazz inhaled and took a quick mental inventory of herself. Her back and elbow hurt where she struck the ground, but nothing severe. Then again, she'd never been shot before, so how would she know? "I don't feel any major pain, so I'm gonna say no."

More voices pierced the air, mostly male.

"What the hell's goin' on out here?"

"I thought I heard a gun."

"Someone get shot?"

Wolf stood up and extended his hand to Jazz. "Real smart. Bullets flying and everyone comes out to see."

She accepted the offer and rose on wobbling legs. Thoughts raced through her brain at warp speed, and she felt her body start shaking. *I hope Liz is okay. If she dies, would the children go into the foster system? Would they come live with me? Why did we get shot at? What would Madge and Bill do without me? Do bullets hurt?* Her synapses misfired and overloaded. The muted roar in her ears took over, and shutdown was imminent.

Wolf cupped her chin and pulled it gently up to make her face him. She noticed his hand was warm against her cold skin. It helped her focus and brought her back to the present. "Stay with me, babe. Keep it together for a little while longer, yeah?"

She nodded against his grip, her eyes boring into his.

"That's my girl."

Officer Denny took over. "Nothing to see here folks, just some kids with Daddy's guns firing into the air to make trouble. Go back to your business or go home." To Wolf, he gave a pointed look and stated, "You realize I'm gonna hafta report this. Get statements and shit. You still want me to arrest the banshee?"

Wolf inhaled through his nose at the nuisance. "No, I'll let her off the hook this time. Mind talking to the ladies tomorrow? I want to get them home."

The uniformed man gave a sharp nod. "I can do that."

Some men grumbled and went back into the club. Others started walking down the street to cars or the few blocks to residences. Officer Denny detained a few and took out his pen and paper to get a few statements while the incident was fresh.

Cam joined Wolf and Jazz, dragging a white-faced, subdued Liz with him. "We can't let this go anymore. This was a direct challenge. We gotta answer back before something else goes down and someone really gets hurt."

Wolf's mouth turned down. "Scrap will call a church meeting 'bout this, probably tomorrow. I wanna know where that Leo fucker is right now."

Cam kept his voice low, but Jazz still heard him. "Took off down the street like a fucking coward. Left everyone in the dust."

Jazz's shaking got worse, and she felt cold inside. She noticed when Wolf placed his arm around her shoulders and tucked her into his side. His heat was welcoming, and she burrowed into him, seeking whatever shelter he offered as he continued to converse with Camshaft. "Show's over for tonight. Everyone goes home. Now. Get Crossman out here and take Liz home."

"What about Candie?"

"I'll deal with her later."

He turned to Jazz. "I need some time to get everyone out and lock up. You're staying with me."

It wasn't a request or an order. It was a statement of fact, or at least that's the way she heard it. He brought her into the club and sat her down on a barstool with a questionable sticky coating.

I'm gonna need a shower.

She watched as Wolf made all the people leave. Only a few protested, but one glance at Wolf's stony face was enough to convince them not to argue.

A tall, voluptuous, near-naked blonde tottered up on glittering heels.

"Hey, Wolf. You okay?"

He gave her such an angry glare that Jazz was sure the woman would be burned. "What the fuck, Candie? You fucking know better than to bring clients or boyfriends into the club."

Her head reared back. "What's the big deal? It's a private room and a private dance."

"Not that private. You want to do a side gig, that's your business, but you take it to the hourly motel down the street. You don't give out blow jobs here in the club."

Candie fluffed her hair indignantly. "Why should

I rent a room? He's my new man, so he doesn't have to pay for a room too."

"There are rules for a reason, Candie. If you fuck up the business, we get problems. We don't want problems."

The adrenaline that had kept Jazz up so far was waning, and her whole body was losing momentum. Sleep beckoned, and she hoped this night would be over soon. Her eyes blinked, unfocused, at the arguers, and it was getting harder to keep them open.

"If it's all the same to you, I'd like to go home now," she said.

"Just a few more minutes, babe," Wolf replied, then turned back to the blonde. "Candie, get your ass dressed and get out."

"What about my tips?"

"You'll cash out tomorrow. Now go!"

Candie made a throaty protest sound and strolled through the back of the club.

Wolf hurried to Jazz. "Think you can stay on my bike long enough to get home?"

She nodded sleepily. "I'll try."

The ride was eerily quiet as they made their way over the bridge and through the streets to Jazz's neighborhood. Perhaps she would remember and appreciate the significance of being on the back of his bike one day, but at the moment, she was too damn tired. The helmet prevented her from resting completely against his body, but he insisted she put the heavy thing on. Wolf put on safety glasses but went bareheaded, as he only had the one with him tonight. Pennsylvania laws allowed for that with his experience and age.

Freya greeted them at the door with mews and demands for cuddles and treats. Jazz picked her up and took her downstairs into the kitchen area to dump dry food into a bowl. She dragged herself back upstairs to find Wolf had taken off his jacket and boots.

"You've been avoiding me all week. Why?" His voice didn't rise in pitch or volume, but there was a command behind it that meant he wouldn't give up without an answer.

She took a breath. *I don't want to be trouble. I like you. I don't know how you feel about me. I'm scared.* "I like trouble." *Dammit!* "I scare you." *Just shut up, Jazz, before you make it worse!*

"I'm staying the night," he announced.

Jazz's stomach went all squishy, and she wrapped her arms around herself to keep it together. "Okay."

He frowned. "I don't think you understand, babe. I'm not leaving. I'm gonna be in your bed.

With you. For the rest of the night. Is that a problem?"

Realization dawned on her. "Oh. Um… no… I'm okay with you here?"

He raised an eyebrow. "Babe, I can't answer that question for you."

"I'm okay with you here."

It took only three strides for him to reach her. His hands came up to seize either side of her face, and a second later, his mouth slammed down on hers.

The kiss was wild. Jazz's senses pushed into overdrive as she opened to him. His tongue swept in possessively, and her brain short-circuited with all the electricity that shot through her like a Tesla coil. Her world tilted, and she realized Wolf had just lifted her against him. Her legs came up to wrap around his waist, and before she could think, they were in her bedroom, and she was on the bed with Wolf standing over her, ripping his shirt over his head.

She got a glimpse of all his tattooed glory before he leaned down and kissed her again. His hands moved to rid her of her T-shirt. She hadn't put on a bra before taking off to the club, and her small breasts were bared to his gaze. He cupped one and squeezed it as he lifted it to his mouth. Jazz watched in fascination as he sucked the tip between his lips. The sensation rushed like a waterfall from her nipple down between her legs and flooded her with heat. He wasn't gentle with her, but it wasn't painful. It was stunning.

He switched sides, treating her other breast with as much attention. His hand moved to pluck and tease so both nipples were stimulated. Jazz heard moaning and realized the sounds were coming from her.

"Wolf," she started to say, then stopped as she didn't have words to describe what she was thinking or feeling.

"I got you, babe."

He didn't hesitate as he pulled the galaxy-patterned leggings from her body and parted her thighs. Jazz had a brief moment of panic when she remembered she hadn't shaved her legs in days, but that didn't last as his mouth came down on her and zeroed in on her clit.

She remembered as a kid taking a dare with Hugo to put a nine-volt battery against their tongues. They took turns and laughed at the shocks. Multiply that by ten and that might come close to what she experienced under Wolf. She jumped at the electric jolt between her legs. How did he know how to do that?

She arched at the unfamiliar sensation, and he grabbed her hips to hold her still.

He was merciless, driving her higher and higher up a cliff she'd never climbed. It was thrilling and overwhelming. She had an idea of what lay at the end, but this was unknown and scary. Then it hit like a roller coaster peaking at the top just before a steep, fast descent, and she fell with a long keening cry as she was unable to stop it or slow it down. Her legs quivered and shook as her core spasmed in uncontrolled waves.

It felt surreal as Wolf raised himself over her body. She watched as he took a plastic square from his wallet before shedding his jeans. His cock was hard and proud. She noticed the wide mushroom head had a darker color, and a drop of fluid appeared at the tip before he rolled the thin latex over it. Then he came down on her and kissed her, driving his tongue into her mouth. She tasted herself on his lips, sweet and salt and musk.

He lined himself up and pushed inside her body in one firm stroke. She gasped in surprise. She knew he wasn't a small man, but she didn't expect this level of discomfort.

"Christ," he growled as he held himself rigidly still. "You a virgin?"

"No?"

He paused, his eyes darkening. "Baby, do not tease me. Either you are or you aren't." A fine sheen of sweat gleamed on his handsome face. He didn't withdraw, but the sting of his entry faded. His body shook with the effort of holding back.

Jazz swallowed. This conversation was awkward as hell with her lying there spread-eagle and penetrated so completely. "I... I had an encounter in college when I was twenty. I thought I was the last virgin on campus, and I had this friend who helped me out with it."

"What do you mean?"

She thought the heat from her face would leave burns. "I made a decision, kinda spur of the moment, and... well... just got rid of my virginity one afternoon during exams. It wasn't at all what the books said it was. It hurt like hell, and he had a lot of trouble with... he didn't last very long. We did it a few more times, but neither of us enjoyed it, or at least I didn't, so... um... that's it."

He stared. "You didn't enjoy it?"

She shook her head.

"So, you've never had an orgasm? Not even making yourself come?"

Jazz covered her face with her hands trying to

shield herself from embarrassment. "I've never really thought about doing it again, but the last time you were here, you touched me, and... I... um... kinda liked it." Could her face get any redder? "I liked... what you just did too."

"So, that was your first orgasm?"

"Yes?"

He let her question/answer go. "That's good, because I'm gonna do it again." He flexed inside her, and her eyes opened wide at the unfamiliar sensation. "I'm gonna do this again too. A lot. This is your only chance to tell me to stop, 'cause I'm going to give you another orgasm, and then I'm gonna come myself. In case you haven't guessed yet, this is not a one-shot deal. When I said I was staying—" He leaned down closer, his breath puffing against her lips. "—I meant I was *staying*."

Her belly hummed with energy, ready to be released. This was Wolf, the man she had crushed on for years. Naked. In her bed. Merged deep inside her.

Did she want this?

Yes. Yes, she did. More than anything in her life, she wanted this.

"Aye, aye, captain."

WOLF STARED DOWN AT THE SMALL FORM curled against him. Her bed wasn't very big, and they barely fit on its frame. Jazz's blue hair lay across his bicep and he fingered a lock of it as she slept securely in his arms. Her light snoring proved to him how much he'd worn her out, and he smiled in satisfaction. He'd held himself back as long as he could, but when she bowed up under him and he felt her pussy spasm around his cock, he let go and had the most gratifying experience he ever remembered. No guile, no subterfuge, no strings, just pure unencumbered pleasure. Something that was rare in his world. He was sure she would be sore tomorrow, and he made a mental note to be extra gentle with her.

For the longest time, he'd found her awkwardness around him cute. He'd known she had a crush on him and was both flattered and amused. Then he'd discovered her side hobby with the scammer thing. He was impressed with her smarts and her willingness to help people. Her work ethic and care for the people around her despite having a seriously unsupportive family was remarkable. There were depths to her character he had yet to plumb, and he looked forward to seeing what was next. It also helped that she was a sci-fi nut.

He glanced over at the bookcase in the bedroom.

Classic hardcovers mixed in with well-loved paper-backs. Philip K. Dick, Douglas Adams, Hugh Howey, some authors he recognized, and some he didn't. Wolf smiled as he thought about the coming months. It would be interesting for sure. He could see them reading and discussing their favorite books together, watching movies with popcorn, then going at it like rabbits until neither of them could move. It was a nice picture, one that never appealed to him before, but he found he liked it.

He liked it a lot.

Yeah, the others in the club would probably make fun of him, but he really didn't care. Jazz fit him in more ways than he ever thought a woman could, and for the first time, he saw a future that included someone else.

Jazz stirred and frowned. "Need to put more chalk on the grill."

Wolf pressed his lips together to keep from laughing and waking her. So, she was a sleep-talker too? Excellent.

"What are you cooking, baby?" he whispered.

"Parachutes." She rolled over and snorted.

With a grin, he snuggled her close.

Yeah, this lone wolf wanted to be domesticated.

17

The entire club waited silently. The leadership had become so lax that church meetings were rare, but enough members were incensed after the drive-by shooting that they demanded this gathering. The Knights didn't have a formal table or gavel, and there were no Robert's Rules to follow. Still, most of the grumbles were held back as everyone looked to Scrap for leadership.

Wolf had his doubts that he would do much. The older man was tired and ready to let someone else make the hard decisions. The problem was, no one in the club was willing to step into that role. Maybe Quillon could fill the void, but did he want to? Scrap's old lady left years ago, and he had no other family as far as anyone knew. Was Quillon's wife, Tracie, ready to be the first queen of the MC?

Wolf shifted his stance—he preferred standing, as the meeting area was next to the main stage—and frowned at the lackluster attitude of the group. Baghouse was enraged and cursing a blue streak under his breath. Melter was picking at a dry cuticle and seemingly unaffected by the shooting. Camshaft, Quillon, and Wolf appeared to be the most concerned.

Scrap finally spoke as he tapped his fingers on the arm of his throne. "I'd say those jagoffs are nothin' to worry about. They're just stupid shits playin' in the streets n'at. Nothin' to worry about."

Wolf couldn't believe his ears. Neither could many of the other members. Camshaft and Crossman glanced at each other in disbelief, and Quillon made a chuffing noise as he closed his eyes and shook his head.

"What the fuck?" Baghouse started, his eyes going wide. "Are you stupid or somethin'?"

Melter scoffed. "Show some fuckin' respect!"

"I'll show some goddamn respect when we get off our fuckin' asses and take care of business!"

Melter jumped to his feet. "You want me to take care of business here, asswipe?"

"Enough!" Scrap roared, temporarily halting the infighting. "We don't have the manpower or the money for a fuckin' street war. When was the last time we had a prospect? Huh? The last one was Crossman, and that's been what? Five years?"

Wolf folded his arms. Scrap had a good point. They didn't have the numbers or the financial backers of the Slaggers. But did that mean they had to give up their territory? Sell the strip joint? Dissolve the club completely?

When he joined the Iron City Knights years ago, they had a reputation as being a tough but fair group. You didn't fuck with them and they wouldn't fuck with you, but if you did, watch out. That had gone by the wayside, and all Wolf saw now was a group of old men coasting on past glories and ready to retire.

"Point of order." Quillon's low voice cut through the cacophony.

Scrap waved at him to continue, and the members quieted to hear what the man had to say.

"I'm gonna disagree with you, Scrap. No disrespect, but flying bullets are not toys to put away at the end of playtime. Yeah, we think they fired in the air, prolly to scare us. Either that or they really suck at aiming since no one got hurt. This time." He looked the club president in the eye and didn't waver. "There is going to be a next time, and someone *will* get hurt. It's inevitable. Could be a patron. Could be a dancer. Could be one of us, but it's coming unless we stop it now."

Scrap sighed. At one time, the man had been tougher than the steel he made. Now he just looked tired and worn out. "How the fuck are we supposed to do that?"

"We have allies."

Scrap sat back and crossed his arms in front of his chest, stating without words that he didn't like the suggestion. "You think we're that weak we gotta ask someone for help?"

"Yes." Quillon didn't back down. "I got a woman I love, work I enjoy, and a club I respect. One is threatened, all three are threatened. My life is good, and I want to keep it that way, whatever it takes."

Wolf jumped in before Scrap could work up a head of steam. "Who did you have in mind?"

"I spoke to Tower from the Miners' Sons MC. He's got a few younger men who are restless and don't want to spend half their lives underground. They might even patch over if they like city life instead of rural coal mining. Tower said if we got jobs for them and a place to live, he'd send them our way to test the fit, so to speak."

An idea formed in Wolf's head. One he loved. "My landlady is moving to her daughter's place in Florida for the summer. She might even stay there permanently. I can speak to her about letting those guys stay at her place. Two bedrooms on the main floor and my apartment on the top floor. Rent is low as long as we keep the place up."

Camshaft spoke up. "Sounds like a plan, but where will you be stayin'?"

Wolf grinned. "I got a spot."

Melter popped his eyes. "Christ on a cracker, you got a woman?"

"Yeah."

If he wasn't sure before, he was now. The short answer cemented Jazz's place in his life more firmly than he realized. The thought of being with her in that odd little house should have been abhorrent to him. Instead, he was already mentally sifting through his stuff to see what he'd bring over and what he'd leave behind.

Melter whooped and slapped his thigh. "Fuck me sideways, you got laid last night!"

Anger flared in Wolf. "How much did those dental implants you got last year set you back? If you want to keep them, I suggest you watch your mouth about my woman."

My woman. Damn, those words tasted good on his tongue. Almost as good as Jazz herself.

Based on her messed-up words last night, he could tell she was nervous and unsure. The sex was mind-blowing, but was she ready to trust him and his commitment? He was completely confident she would get there.

Quillon brought the main topic back. "So, do we need a formal vote or what?"

A sea of shrugs and a chorus of "Yeah, sures" and "Whatevers" came from the sparse membership. Wolf frowned at the apathy. It seemed like no one really cared about the future of the club. At one time, the name Iron City Knights meant something. It seemed at this point, the club was dying a slow, quiet death, and no one gave a shit.

"Through the fires of hell, men of steel are forged." The club motto rang in his head like hammers against an anvil. The time would come when they would have to reforge the club. When they did, would the result be a stronger steel or something so weak it would snap in half? Only time would tell.

Quillon waved a hand in the air in a move-on gesture. "Motion carried and approved. Let's get this shit done."

18

"SO, LEO AND LIZ ARE DONE? LIKE permanently?" Hugo asked Jazz as he rolled out a sheet of dough and handed it off to the girl next to him. "Remember how to use the cookie cutter, right? Straight rows."

Hugo had introduced her as Erica, another resident of the group home. She, too, was a person with Down syndrome, but she seemed to struggle more than Hugo. Her eyes focused on the bone-shaped cutter, and she looked uncomprehendingly at the dough before realizing her task. Then she started carefully pressing the tool into the dough in vertical columns.

"That's it. That's perfect. Good job, Erica." Hugo's praise made the girl grin, and she concentrated harder on making the rows as straight as possible. It was slow going, but no one criticized or hurried her.

Jazz took a couple hours away from the coffee shop during the afternoon slowdown to spend a few minutes with her brother and find some sanity. There was something calming about being in his presence and in his kitchen. The simple, methodical, and repetitive baking of the dog treats was soothing to her, and she found order in his world rather than the chaotic mess of her own. One resident mixed the bowls of dough using four ingredients. The measuring cups were color coded so they didn't get mixed up: red for the flour, green for the peanut butter, blue for the applesauce, and yellow for the bone broth. The man poured and stirred, then handed off the mixture to the head supervisor, who used the KitchenAid standing mixer. Bowl after bowl lined up for Hugo to roll out and guide Erica through the cutting process. The next person poked holes in each treat before the second supervisor put them in the big ovens to bake.

"Yes, Leo and Liz are done. I don't think they'll ever get back together," she answered Hugo's question as he lifted the spare dough from the cut cookies and mashed it into the next pile to roll out.

"They don't love each other, so it's good that they

aren't together anymore." Hugo's round face didn't show any emotion one way or another.

"I guess you're right," she commented, then fell silent as the mixer started up. Her body hummed in time with the laboring motor, and she couldn't help but replay last night's events.

Wolf had stayed with her all night, spooning her body and keeping her close. This morning, he woke her much like he'd done the last time he slept in her bed.

"You sore, baby?"

She squirmed as his mouth tugged on one nipple. "I... a little... I... maybe?"

His chuckle tickled against the skin of her abdomen. "I can wait. Besides, I need to get more rubbers. I used up what I had last night." He slid lower. "But just because I'm gonna take a break doesn't mean you have to."

"Yo, sis? What are you thinking about?"

Jazz jolted back to the present and regarded her brother with a shaky smile. "Nothing you need to know about."

"Was it the motorcycle guy?"

She coughed to cover her surprise. "Why would you think that?"

"'Cause he's cool, and he likes you." Hugo grinned

and handed another tray of rolled dough to Erica. "He wants to be your boyfriend."

"How do you know?"

"Duh," he intoned. "He didn't let Mom or Liz say bad stuff about you. That means he likes you." He paused and looked up at his favorite sister. "Don't you like him?"

"Yes. Yes, I do."

"Then you should be his girlfriend."

Jazz wished like hell she could view everything through her brother's eyes. Simple and straightforward. If A equals B and B equals C, then A equals C.

Could it be that easy?

Her phone buzzed, and she saw a new text from the subject of her conversation with Hugo.

> Wolf: The fridge is empty. I'm gonna grab some groceries and cook dinner before work. Grabbed your spare key from the rack. Hope you don't mind. How do you feel about lasagna?

She ignored the invasion of her space and concentrated on his other words. He was getting groceries. *He was getting groceries!*

> Jazz: I like lasagna.

Wolf: What's your favorite coffee in the morning? I noticed you don't have any here.

Jazz: I don't really like coffee. I'm more of a tea person.

Wolf: Your shitting me. You make fancy coffee drinks all day and don't like it yourself?

Jazz: You're. I drink coffee sometimes, but I like hot tea better.

Wolf: You're something else, baby. I'll get some fancy teas, then. See you at the house.

"You're doing that face again," Hugo interrupted.

"That was... um... Wolf. The biker. He's getting groceries and making lasagna for dinner."

Her brother didn't bother to hide his I-told-you-so look. "See? Boyfriend. You're so weird."

19

Summer was making its debut, and heat would be upon the city very soon, but for now, the nights were still cool and comfortable. Jazz sat facing the river on the front deck, which had room enough for a small round table and two folding lounge chairs. Freya's gurgling purr accompanied the river sounds as the cat kneaded her thighs. Jazz lifted a cup and sipped the herbal tea.

The workday had been incredibly long and exhausting. No different from the rest of the past few weeks. No clue how much longer she would be able to keep up with the pace, but Wolf was there every minute.

He also seemed to have moved in—*permanently*. Originally, he told her he needed a place to crash for a little while. That had been two weeks ago. Currently, he was in her shower making use of the new water heater he'd installed earlier that afternoon.

It was admittedly convenient to have him around, as her place needed some care. They often worked at the bakery together, and she rode on the back of his bike there and back.

She wasn't naive enough not to understand what that meant.

Bill was healing, and Madge had started coming back to work more. He was still a long way off from being able to take care of himself, but at least his wife could get the baking done, which was an essential part of their business, and give Jazz a break from the counter.

The cup she held was taken away by a thick finger, and Jazz looked up to see Wolf with a towel wrapped around his hips. He lifted the R2-D2 mug and took a sip. She took note of his grimace, but her eyes were on the tattoo across his rippled abs.

"Don't you find it a bit strange to be known as a top barista, but you don't like coffee?"

Maybe. You're naked. Technically in public. "Maybe naked in public?"

He laughed and bent to place the cup on the table, then brought his face close to hers. "No one is on the greenway, and we're well hidden by all those bushes. Anyone on the river would have to have binoculars to see, and even then, it's quite a distance." His lips brushed over hers. "Want to get naked together out here?"

Yes! "Yes."

He pulled the "I Love Spock" T-shirt over her head and settled his hips between her knees to feast on her breasts. She leaned back and closed her eyes as Freya objected to being dislodged. Wolf lowered his mouth over one nipple, sucked it to a point, and then laved it flat with his tongue. A combination moan and sigh left her as he rolled the other one between his fingers.

He did this a lot, giving her breasts this kind of attention every day. It was one of his favorite foreplay moves, and she had yet to grow tired of it. Would she ever?

During this time of living with him, she no longer had any doubts that he wanted to be with her. His first week, he fixed the running toilet, replaced the leaky faucet in the kitchen, and tightened up the loose railing on the walkway to the street. When she protested, he said that since he'd moved in, he needed to do his fair share of upkeep. The second week, he tore out the ratty carpet and cracked linoleum and refinished the hardwood floor underneath. So far this week, he'd replaced the water heater and some plumbing.

He also made love to her daily.

She had to call it *making love*, because *fucking* or *having sex* didn't fit. Those terms sounded transactional and cold and had nothing to do with the intimate times they spent together. Wolf gave as much as he took, always with care. He asked her how she felt, what she liked, and how far she would go. His respect and communication made her less awkward around him, and for the first time, she knew what it was to be cherished.

Jazz writhed as his hands moved to her hips, and she lifted them in the chair as he peeled down her leggings, taking her underwear with them. He spread her thighs wide to open her bare pussy. He'd shaved it himself just a few nights ago, making it one of the most deeply personal and trusting encounters she'd ever had. His fingers opened her sex, and he drew her distended clit between his lips. Something else she quickly found out was that he loved going down on her. She could be jealous of all the women he'd practiced on before her, but at the moment, she was grateful for their tutelage.

He licked and sucked her at a leisurely pace,

keeping her jerking hips still with his hands. Jazz thought he treated her like an ice cream cone, taking all the time in the world to draw out the flavor. The orgasm he pulled out of her hit hard, and she let out a small scream as the release made her lose control. One thick finger pushed inside her channel just before the first wave hit her, and she cried out in pleasure. Her hands clutched his hair as he finished her with one last twirl of his tongue.

A moment later, he shed his towel and lifted her from the chair. He sat down in her place and pulled her legs over his hips so she straddled him. She balanced herself as the head of his hard cock made contact with her wet, pulsing channel.

"Lean back, baby. I want to watch you take me."

She slid down. Would she ever get tired of the sensation when he first breached her opening and slowly filled the void inside her? Jazz let out a low moan as he guided her movements, found that perfect angle, and steadily stroked it like he was petting her.

"You good, babe?"

She smiled and arched her back to take more. "Yes. Very."

He wet his thumb and pressed it to her clit so each thrust added another layer of sensation. He teased and kept her just under climaxing again until she was ready to scream. When he finally allowed her to come, it was long and so intense that she lost her senses for anything other than the pleasure he gave her. Her core burned with fire as wave after wave crashed over her. He quickly found his climax, too, swelling and then pulsing inside her.

"Christ!" he growled and pulled her down to rest his forehead against hers. Both of them panted at the power of their lovemaking and how it left them both satisfied and relaxed.

"Will it always be like this?" she asked as she ran her hands over his chest and shoulders.

"I don't know, but I don't see it stopping anytime soon." He kissed her before sliding out.

She felt the wetness between her legs then and turned her eyes to him in mild panic. "We didn't use a condom."

She slid off and stretched back on the lounge as he stood and picked up the discarded towel, draping it over his shoulder. "You okay with that? I don't know what you think about having kids, but for the record, I'm not worried if it happens."

That took her by surprise. "You... you want to...?"

He laughed as he bent to scoop her up in his arms. Hers automatically came around his neck as he lifted her against his bare chest and strode through the door. Freya darted inside just as he kicked it shut. "We'll need a bigger house. I don't know if you want to add on to this one or look for something else, but we have time. I'm not going anywhere."

The bedroom wasn't far. He found the bed and laid her on her back with ease as he leaned over her. His fingers traced a pattern on her stomach, and his face grew serious. "All joking aside, I don't know how I feel about what's happening between us, but I can't see a future without you in it. I remember my parents and how they functioned as one unit. They never did anything without the other. Grocery shopping, oil changes, school events—they were always together. I never thought I'd find someone I'd want to be that close to, and now I have."

He spread his fingers and placed his warm palm against her lower abdomen. The touch was both personal and possessive. Jazz bit her lip to keep it from quivering as she said, "You already found out I've had a thing for you for years. It's one of the reasons I liked getting up in the morning to go to the coffee shop. Just to see you come in and ask for a latte and a Danish. Is that crazy?"

His hand moved, stroking over her belly. The arousing heat made her want to squirm. "Not crazy at all. I like where we are. I like how we fit. I like being with you more than I have any other woman in my life. I don't know if this is the lasting kind of love, but it sure feels like it."

Jazz's heart did a pirouette. "Are you saying you… um… love me?"

He shifted himself over her, and she parted her legs to let him settle between them. A second later, he was sliding into her welcoming pussy. "Does this answer your question, babe? If you want to stop to get a condom, that's fine, but we've already put the cart before the horse tonight. We can look into a different birth control if you want, but if you're okay for now, I'd like to risk it one more time."

Jazz had no words. Emotions crowded them out, and she could only nod at the man moving inside her for the second time tonight.

The man she recognized as the only one she would ever love.

20

EDGAR MEDFLIN STARED AT THE DISPLAY CASE of vintage fiber-optic lamps. The sprays of thin plastic spaghetti changed colors at random times, and he found it mesmerizing. Of course, the weed he just tried probably had a lot to do with his current state. The Rainbow Belts strain of pot had him seeing colored arcs in the haze around the slowly rotating clouds of sparkles.

"My people are gonna love this shit," he told the lamps, imagining they approved of his opinion.

His vape store was empty this time of night save for himself and the spinning lamps. The music was a widely eclectic mix, ranging from Gregorian chants, '70s rock, club techno, and Tibetan bowl singing. Bongs and hookahs lined the shelf behind the main counter, along with rows of vape devices and accessories. The store's decor hadn't changed since the '80s and was sadly a little dated, but Edgar didn't care. He had plenty of people who bought fruity vape juices and CBD oils from him. Enough to keep the place open and his side pot business laundered.

Lately, though, he'd been thinking about selling everything and taking his happy ass down to Florida. It was all because that biker gang wouldn't leave him alone. First time the Slaggers came through, they offered a business deal to store and distribute the hard stuff. Crack, meth, fennies, whatever it was, he wasn't interested.

They came back with a bigger offer and a threat: Work with us or lose everything. To make that point, they'd trashed a whole display of mini-waterpipes. Still, Edgar wouldn't play ball with them. Yeah, he dealt a little weed out the back door, but he wasn't a big player in the greater scheme of things, so the cops generally left him alone. Edgar liked it like that and had no intention of upsetting the apple cart. Start dealing in the hard stuff? It was only a matter of time before someone fingered him and his whole world collapsed.

He'd heard from other businesses on this strip that the Slaggers had hit them up, too, either for "protection" money or distribution deals. The Iron City Knights had the titty bar down the street and were also a holdout. Edgar figured they would be the ones to kick the rival bikers out of this area for good. But so far, nothing.

Until the drive-by a week or so ago. Edgar couldn't quite recall what day it happened, but he did remember hearing and seeing the vehicle with the guns shooting into the sky. The incident had him thinking maybe it really was time to sell and move. He had cousins in Florida who spent their days on the beach and their nights running the beach stores that sold tourist shit.

"That could be kinda cool."

He wasn't sure why he was talking to himself. A giggle came out of his throat.

"Damn, I'm freakin' high as fuck," he informed the lamps with a nod.

He noticed the black sky outside. Time was relative, and at the moment, he had no idea if it was just after sunset or just before sunrise. Either way, he decided he was hungry.

"Munchies suck."

He thought about the soft pretzels he had in the freezer. Just needed to nuke in the microwave for two minutes, but he'd have to leave the store unattended while he ambled back to the office. Instead, he unwrapped an expired Tastykake and crammed half of it into his bearded mouth.

Prolly got crumbs in my facebush, he thought as he brushed at them.

The sudden crash of glass startled him, and he sucked the wad of masticated dough into his windpipe. Air became a precious commodity as he started choking and tried to dislodge the blocking food.

Death by butterscotch krimpet.

But he was wrong.

It was the bomb that killed him.

21

Wolf and Camshaft watched the inspectors sift through the rubble that was left from the exploded vape shop. The smell of ash still coated the air as the men in suits poked through the debris.

"Bomb." Officer Denny sidled up to the two bikers and joined them in their observations. "Homemade, but more than a Molotov cocktail. Poor fucker was prolly high when he bought it."

Wolf's face remained impassive. The coroner's van had already come to collect Ed's twisted, burned remains. Wolf never had an issue with the man. They weren't friends, but he didn't wish him dead. "Any clues to prove who did it?"

Denny sighed. "Nothing so far we can use. No traffic cameras on the streets. No witnesses." He huffed as one worker lifted a chunk of wall. "We know who did this, but we got *bupkis* to go on."

Camshaft spoke. "I'm surprised the buildings on either side weren't damaged."

"Targeted explosion," Wolf said with a grim voice. "One of the Slaggers either has demolition experience or was in the military."

Denny raised an eyebrow. "How do you know that?"

"Walls collapsed inward."

Wolf's mind had already moved beyond the ruined headshop and its dead owner. If it was the Slaggers, they'd upped their game. Someone was backing them, as there was no way their club could get the explosives needed to level a building. One of their larger allies? A bigger club? Drug cartel like Baghouse said?

If the Knights didn't step up now, there might not be another chance. It also might be too late already.

He turned away from the sight. "You get any intel, feel free to share. I expect this isn't the last building or business that's gonna go down."

Denny made a hum of confirmation and stayed in his spot as the two bikers walked down the street to the strip club.

Very few dancers worked during the day, but

there were always a few patrons in the late afternoon. Portia was on the raised stage, but her performance was lackluster, as only three men were there, sipping beer and staring at her bare breasts. None of them gave a hint about tipping.

Scrap and Baghouse sat in their usual spots with a game of chess in front of them. Two of the crossover prospects swept the floors, and another one was manning the bar.

Wolf held his temper in check as he addressed the president. "We need a church meeting."

Scrap moved a knight. "What the fuck for?"

"I just came from the head shop, or what was left of it. They had to scrape Ed off the floor. We can't keep ignoring this shit."

"What the fuck are we supposed to do about it? Just leave it."

Wolf gestured to the new recruits. "Tower sent us his three best recruits. We need to use them for more than cleaning and serving drinks. We have to get more weapons and ammo stockpiled. Set up patrols around the perimeters. Make our colors stand out. If we find any Slaggers in our territory, we send a message that they need to stay away or else."

"We do that, blood's gonna be spilt."

"Blood's already been spilt."

Scrap slammed his hand on the table, making the chess pieces fall and scatter. "Last time I looked, I was still the leader of this club. I said leave it!"

Wolf clamped down on his rising temper. "You can stick your head in the ground, but that doesn't mean the world stops." His tone sharpened, and his words spat out like verbal punches. "The Slaggers will come back, and when they do, they'll bring more than bullets fired in the air. You own this building, but no one owns the club."

Baghouse grumbled as he set the pieces up for another round. "He's right. We gotta handle those fuckin' jagoffs soon."

"Fuck off and make your move," Scrap grumbled. "We ain't doing shit."

Wolf felt the dismissal and fumed with suppressed fury. Quillon was at his forge and would be incommunicado for the day. Camshaft and Crossman were at the machine shop or sleeping, as both of them were on duty tonight. He had no backup other than Baghouse, and he was full of hot air most of the time. The man could spew all the attitude, but when it came down to making a decision or stepping up, he was absent.

Wolf stalked away from the stubborn leader. When did Scrap lose his balls? The club dysfunction worsened every damn day, and no one had the guts to fix it. Visions of Ed's blackened corpse floated in his mind as he stormed down the short hall. He happened to glance in room two and stopped dead at the sight.

Candie wasn't giving a blow job this time. She was bent over and taking it from behind as that fucker Leo pounded into her.

Rage filled Wolf, and this time, he let it loose. The doorknob embedded itself in the wall as he flung it open. "What the fuck do you think you're doing?"

Leo squealed and fell back, tripping over the tangle of work pants around his knees.

Candie's scream was more of outrage than embarrassment from getting caught. "What the hell, Wolf? You can't come in here while I've got someone with me!"

"I'm sick of this shit, Candie. You know damn well not to bang your clients here. You want to make money whoring yourself, that's your business, but it does not come in here."

She remained bent over, not caring in the least that her bare pussy was showing wide open. The harsh words didn't faze her. "Leo only gets thirty minutes on his lunch break, and that asshole at the motel charges by the hour."

Wolf couldn't believe what he was hearing. "So pay for the hour."

She had the nerve to roll her eyes. "That makes no sense." She stood up, unconcerned by her naked state nor Leo's scrambling movements as he righted his clothes. "Why should he pay for a whole hour when my room here is just as good, and no one is around anyway?"

Wolf's anger ratcheted higher. He pointed a thick finger at Leo. "Get out." His growl was low, but the menace was unmistakable.

The man paled and didn't bother to say anything to his girlfriend. He just turned tail and ran.

Wolf turned back to Candie, who had crossed her arms under her breasts, plumping them up even more. "That's not the point and you know it. This is not your private room or your personal business to do whatever the fuck you want to do." He pointed to the door. "Go get dressed, get your shit, and get the fuck out!"

Her eyes widened, and she dropped her arms to place her hands on her hips. "Are you firing me?"

"Yes, I am."

She laughed as if he'd told her the funniest joke ever. "You can't do that. The men who come here come to see *me* dance. They won't come if you fire me."

Wolf's expression turned nasty. "You think that, eh? Who in this fucking city hasn't seen your tits already? Give it a week and some younger new dancers will fill those seats no problem."

"Fuck you!"

"Been there. Done that. Not worth a repeat."

She screeched and came at him with her fingernails curled into claws. Wolf caught her wrists and held her back. "You have two choices. Take the five minutes I'll give you to get dressed, or don't. Either way, you're leaving."

Candie's face twisted into a raging mask of hatred. "Scrap won't let you do this!"

"Scrap's not the manager here. I am. Four minutes or you're out on your bare ass."

She jerked back, freeing herself. Her breasts heaved as she puffed in frustration. Wolf braced for another attack. Instead, she sneered and tossed her head back in imperial disgust. "You're gonna regret this. My fans will demand my return." She pointed a talon at his face. "I'll be back on that stage in a week."

"Three minutes." He could see the frustration on Candie's snarling face. This was a power play through and through. The woman clearly wanted to fight more, maybe throw something or have a screaming tantrum. Candie was seldom told no, and for years she'd gotten away with shit, mostly because Wolf hadn't taken a big enough stand. He felt a tiny bit guilty about that, as he should have stopped this long ago, but it wasn't like the woman hadn't been warned time and time again.

Tears spilled over Candie's false lashes, and she dashed them away, leaving a black smear under her eyes. "It's that hippie girl you're fucking. She's got you thinking about commitments and houses and kids. She's just a novelty. People like you and me? We're the real deal."

"Two minutes."

"You bastard!" Candie's face changed again. She lashed out, and Wolf didn't block her this time. Her nails caught his cheek and left two shallow red lines just above his beard.

"Time's up." He seized her wrist and pulled her from the room. Scrap and Baghouse glanced up from their game to watch as Wolf dragged an enraged cursing Candie through the club, completely naked.

Camshaft walked in the front door, and his eyes nearly popped from his head at the sight. "What the fuck is going on?"

Wolf didn't stop moving. "Grab Candie's stuff

from her locker, yeah? She doesn't work here anymore."

Unlike the dancer, Camshaft didn't question him and hurried to the dressing room.

The street wasn't full of people, but there was definitely an audience when Wolf dragged Candie to the concrete sidewalk. He dropped her arm and blocked her entrance back into the club.

"You're hurting me!" she shrieked.

"I'm not touching you. I did not throw you down or hit you or push you."

"You assaulted me!"

He pointed to the blood on his cheek. "Who assaulted whom?"

"Go fuck yourself!"

Camshaft appeared with the contents of Candie's locker and wordlessly tried to hand everything to the spitting woman. She slapped it out of his hand. "Kiss my ass!"

"Suit yourself. I'm done." Wolf turned and went back into the club. Camshaft followed and closed the door, muffling the still-cursing woman. Scrap and Baghouse were staring at the two younger men.

Wolf spoke coldly. "I fired Candie. Either of you have a problem with that?"

Scrap dropped his eyes to the board. "Bitch making trouble again?"

"Yeah."

The older man picked up a bishop and placed it on another square. "Your move."

Wolf's cheek stung where Candie's nails had made contact. He left the men to their game and made his way to the men's bathroom and the first aid kit.

He cursed as he applied the alcohol wipe to his face, the burn fueling his bad mood. The club was falling apart, and there was nothing he could do about it.

Nothing but call a vote and replace Scrap as president.

Wolf stared at his reflection and frowned deep enough to carve lines around his mouth. That was the most radical step he or anyone else in the club could take, and once it was made, there was no going back. The challenger would either replace Scrap or leave the club.

Wolf tossed the used wipe into the trash as Camshaft entered the bathroom. "You okay, man?"

"Yeah. I need to get out of here and catch some rack time. You got this covered until I get back later?"

"Sure. What do I do if Candie comes back?"

"Call me or Denny, or just kick her out."

Wolf left the club. Thankfully, there was no sign of Candie anywhere, and he was able to get to his bike in peace. He thought about going over to the bakery and seeing Jazz for a few minutes—something about her presence made him feel better—but sleep was calling him more. He mounted up and sent her a quick text.

> Wolf: I need to grab some Zs. Heading home soon. You need me to get anything on the way?

It took a few minutes for her to reply, but when it came, part of the tension in his body relaxed.

> Jazz: Getting low on toilet paper. Mi casa es su casa?

He grinned at the message. *Baby, you have no idea what you're in for.*

> Wolf: Is that a question?

> Jazz: Mi casa es su casa or whatever.

22

Cornelius sat heavily in his computer chair and leaned back into the thick padding. He'd designed it specifically for his round body so when he started a marathon session, he could do so in complete comfort. The bank of monitors sat in front of him, glowing with their screen savers. This was the most powerful machine he'd ever built, and very few people in his immediate circle knew about it or could understand it.

It didn't really bother him that his closest friends didn't know this part of his life. His people accepted and loved him for himself, not his hacker talents. He was okay with that.

The screens came to life as he booted up his massive system. His fingers danced over the keyboard, barely skimming the buttons as he called up and hooked into the dark web. Streams of information flowed into the rolling feed of one monitor while real-time calls appeared on others. One smaller screen showed pictures of the space around his cabin. The place was isolated, but with his satellite setup, he had unlimited bandwidth and access. It was fast.

Cornelius placed the headset over his ears and swung the microphone down to rest in front of his mouth. The voice modulator kicked on and made him sound like a confused old man.

"Hello? I was told to call this number about my son. I got an email that he was in trouble."

The voice at the other end of the phone started a typical script. "This is the European Police department. Your son has been arrested for..."

Cornelius played along without amusement. At one time, messing with scammers was entertainment, but now it was more of a mission. Too many people had lost money to these criminals, and even more, they had lost trust and faith in humanity. The level of personal violation was off the charts, along with the helplessness and despair that there was nothing that could be done. Justice was a fickle bitch; he'd learned that a long time ago.

Cornelius continued to lead the scammer on with

a promise of a big payoff and then killed his entire system. Jazzyhands was really good at this particular schtick and had destroyed many scammers. She'd been off and on lately, but he wasn't too worried, as she checked in enough that he knew she was okay. Her life had taken a different turn as her workload had increased at the coffee shop, and she now had a boyfriend.

The people who hadn't checked in concerned him. Of all the scam-shielders, he was the only one who'd learned who they were. He didn't stalk anyone or interfere in their lives, but he kept tabs on them like a guardian from time to time. Glyndathegood had been out for a while, but he knew the woman had a nasty divorce happening, plus she had other identities she used online. One of them he knew about was CatLady50, but that was more of her personal ID. She'd been offline for weeks now as Glynda. Cornelius pulled up his log records and swore. It had been five weeks since she logged in under either of those names.

A frisson of worry drifted down his spine. Rumors on some of the chat threads circled around some very rich and very pissed-off people who wanted revenge on whoever crippled their network. Cornelius had hoped the whole mess would blow over, but it didn't seem to be going in that direction. He'd sent warnings to the other shielders but hadn't heard any scuttlebutt in a while.

Instead of throwing out his hook for another scammer, he scanned the web for information. It didn't take long for him to find it, and when he did, that worry expanded into full-blown fear.

"Ms. Lynn Farthing, a counselor at Raeford High School, was found dead in a luxury suite at the Radisson West hotel. It appears she drowned in the room's private Jacuzzi after having a number of drinks with a guest at the hotel bar. Ms. Farthing was recently divorced from her husband of twenty-five years and, according to her coworkers, had become increasingly depressed. The coroner has ruled her death an accidental suicide. The room was booked under an international corporation. The police have not yet been able to identify the man she was with."

Cornelius watched the report twice. His mouth pressed into a grim line as his fingers flew over the keyboard, clicking and searching. An article popped up in Texas.

"The University of Texas is reeling from the sudden death of Mark Masters, an engineering student who was set to graduate this year. Witnesses at the Burger Spot diner report that he started seizing while he was eating lunch and passed out. The paramedics were unable to revive him. Although his tox screen was negative, sources say this looked like death from a drug overdose."

"Shit," Cornelius said aloud as he expanded his search. Another report popped up of a man in Canada who died in his apartment under mysterious circumstances. By all indications, he'd suffocated, but it was unknown how it happened.

One by one, the scam-shielders were being picked off. Why? Cornelius's mind immediately thought of the massive network that had collapsed recently. He was sure Jazzyhands brought them down. Those gargantuan call centers had fallen and hadn't recovered yet. Probably never would. Millions, perhaps billions, were lost, and several legit businesses had been affected. It was both impressive and scary as hell that a single person had that kind of talent to create something so destructive. If Jazzyhands wasn't such a good person, there's no telling how much damage she could do.

A movement caught Cornelius's eye. It was brief, just a blip at the edge of his home security screen, but it was enough for his fear to grow cold and morph into anger. He picked up his cell phone and pulled up a number. The phone rang twice before it was answered.

"What's up, Bruiser?"

"Hey, Table. I got company at my place, and I don't think it's the good kind. Mind gettin' me some help?"

"Mute and Dodge are here. You want me to text Stud and Forge?"

Cornelius, aka Bruiser, said, "That's a good idea. Come armed. Whoever's out there knows my cameras' blind spots."

"Shit, brother, are you being targeted?"

"Seems like it."

"On the way."

Bruiser strained his eyes for any more movement. His cabin was eerily quiet, and his hand hovered over the button that would blaze the lights all around his home. They were ranged at 120 lumens, which was enough to cause temporary blindness that could last from a few minutes to several hours. He'd used them only once before when a past two-legged intruder thought his cabin would be easy pickings. The powerful lights plus some well-placed buckshot dissuaded that notion. Bruiser had a feeling he would need more than buckshot this time.

Another motion in the dark close to his deck. He

sensed it more than saw it. His fingers descended to hit the banks of lights at the same time a barely audible *chink* sounded in the air. Bruiser looked down to see a small red spot appear on his chest. One that slowly spread into a blooming flower.

"Oh, fuck, no."

23

A *Star Wars* movie was playing, the lights from the screen dancing gently around the room. Wolf thought it was *Rogue One* but wasn't sure, as neither he nor Jazz paid much attention to it. When he came home, he found her working on her computer for the inventory program she hosted and listening to movies for background noise. No makeup, hair in a loose pile on her head, and glasses perched on her nose, she'd looked up and smiled at him in a genuine warm welcome.

No duplicity.

No fakeness.

No manipulations or lies.

Just pure joy at his presence.

Fuck, how much time had passed before he'd

recognized the happiness that was right in front of him?

"Almost done?"

Her answer was to close the program and move into his arms. A minute later, they were on the bed, her legs spread as he feasted on her. Her moans and cries as he teased her over and over again were music to his ears. She didn't hold back, showing him the pleasure he gave her. He never tired of her taste, her sounds, feeling her come on his tongue and around his cock, her very essence, and all that made her the perfect woman for him.

A lifetime wouldn't be long enough.

Now, they lay cuddled on the bed, still naked with him on his back and her half on, half off him. He traced random patterns over her shoulders as the movie continued.

"I guess you had a rough day?" she asked as her own fingers ran over the details of his ink.

"You could say that. I had to fire Candie."

Her touch stilled. "Oh?"

"She crossed the line too many times. Ignored the rules and policies until I couldn't let it go anymore. Only so far you can push before you come up against a wall."

"I'm sorry?"

"Not your problem, baby. She started it. I finished it. I had to do that a lot when I was military."

Her fingers started back up, running along the inked lines of his chest. "You said you studied engineering, like robots and stuff. Is that what you did in the Army?"

He hesitated. Not many people knew about this part of his life. He only shared part of it with Go-Kart one drunken night a few years ago. But if he wanted to build something with this woman, at some point she would need to know his history, right?

The real question in his mind came to the forefront. Would she leave him when she found out what he had been?

He took a breath. "I went to school on a shooting scholarship. Rifle team. I was the top dog with a higher accuracy at long range than anyone else. National champion. The problem was, the money I got was only good for the first year. The other three would be on me with loans that were high enough in the six-figure range that I'd never have a hope of paying them off. Uncle Sam offered me a solution with the GI Bill. Someone there recognized my talent and offered me a serious amount of money for a serious position."

"What was it?"

He bit his lip. "The military had a use for my particular set of skills. I was a long-range sniper primarily in Afghanistan and Iraq. Some combat, but mostly assigned targets."

"You killed people. Like an assassin?"

He closed his eyes. "Bingo."

Her fingers stopped their movements again. "A lot?"

Her question rang in his head. "Yeah. I don't hold any records or any special awards. I followed orders and did what I was told to do. That's it."

"Oh."

That one syllable could have more than one meaning. "Oh" as in shrugging off his past like it was just another phase, or "Oh" as in "I just realized the kind of man I have in my house and bed," or "Oh, I don't want to be with a murderer, no matter what the reason."

"But you're not a sniper anymore."

"I haven't picked up a gun since I got out. I don't have one for the club or at my house. Not while riding either."

"Oh."

That short word was driving him a little crazy.

"Um... did you... like it?"

He sighed and closed his eyes. "I didn't have some

big revelation over my kills. There wasn't some kid or puppy or person who gave me a guilty conscience and made me regret my job. To me, they were targets. Nothing more. I had no feelings for them. *That* was the problem."

He swallowed as he opened his eyes and stared at the ceiling. "I had no feelings for anyone or anything. If a buddy of mine died in battle, so what? We were there to die. Pain was an annoyance, not an indicator of something wrong. I got my orders. Set my sights. Pulled the trigger. It didn't matter who it was, I'd take them out. No questions."

"Did you… women or children or just bad guys?"

"I never questioned an order."

Silence filled the room with white noise, and for a few moments, he didn't move or breathe.

"I was in for eight years. When I got out, there wasn't any big fanfare or any offer for me to stay. I was a shell. I had no emotions. I didn't care. Someone could drop on the sidewalk in a death spiral and I would keep walking past."

"Like in *The Vampire Diaries*, when they turned off their emotions and became killing machines."

"I never saw that show, but it sounds about right. Living, dying, it was all the same to me. I had no love for anyone. Not my family. Not my wife. No one."

He swallowed. "Darcy, my ex, told me I was a machine. I'd eat, work, and fuck. That was it. I don't remember ever loving her or why we got married. She was both a convenience and an annoyance. I remember her screaming at me over what I thought was stupid shit, like getting the wrong bread from the store or not taking her out for dinner. I think now, she was just trying to get my attention. As much as I'd like to say she was the bitch from hell, when it comes down to it, it was me who was the problem."

Jazz stayed silent for a moment. Long enough to make Wolf wonder if she was thinking about her words or plotting her escape. When she did speak, her voice was heavy. "So, what turned you back on again?"

He let out a long breath. "Corny as it sounds, it was the Knights that saved me. Brought me back to myself, so to speak. I wandered around a bit before moving back here. No plans or anything concrete, but this is where my dad lived, worked, and died. Pittsburgh was home to me at one time, and I figured it was as good as any other. Bill was a coworker of my dad's, so there was still a connection. I met Quillon at a rally. We got a couple of beers, and he told me about the Knights. They were a strong club at one time, and that appealed to me."

Jazz slid a hand across Wolf's abdomen. He found relief and encouragement that she didn't pull away from him. He took it and threaded his fingers between hers. "Have you ever found a group of people that just fit? Like-minded or broken, or they just needed you? That's how I felt about the Knights. It's a mess now, but it's like I'm grounded with them. I have a purpose. There's something to build up, not tear down. They need that, and I need that too. Make sense, or am I just rambling now?"

She squeezed him. "I get that. I'm glad you found a place. It's kinda like me and the shielders. I've always been the family misfit, and the shielders welcomed me, bugs and all. It's not so cool what you had to go through and what you did, but I understand everyone has a past. The Wolf back then is not the Wolf I have in my bed now. I hope I can have a little piece of the future."

His eyes grew moist, and he closed them to keep any tears from falling. They still trickled down from the corners. "You're not just a piece of my world, Jazz. You're all of it."

24

JAZZ PUT AWAY THE FRESHLY WASHED MUGS and wiped down the counter. Her sleep pattern had always been irregular, but the hours were taking a real toll on her now. Bill's recovery was slower than expected, but at least it was moving forward. Madge was running herself to death trying to keep up with the bakery and take care of him. Jazz worked all the hours she could, but it just wasn't enough. Wolf came when he could, but with all the shit going down with the club, his time was also strained.

Jazz yawned and glanced at the time. Three thirty. Two and a half more hours to go. Madge was at home with Bill for the afternoon. Two regular patrons were in their usual chairs clicking away at computers. It was the kind of day she liked. Calm and easy. She had to check on her inventory program, but so far there weren't any glitch alerts, so a quick look-see for maintenance was all that was needed. Wolf was at the Attic all night, so perhaps she could sleep for a change.

A smile spread across her face as she thought about Wolf. His appetites were voracious, and she found herself opening to him on a daily basis. Of course, she didn't mind in the least, as she enjoyed the variety of pleasures he gave her and the ones she gave back. He was more experienced than she was, and that bothered her a bit, but she decided she was reaping the benefits of his developed talents. Afternoon, morning, evening, night, it didn't matter—he took her whenever they were together. Sometimes it was fast and furious, hurtling her into rapid-fire orgasms as many times as he could before he came. Other times, he drew it out, making her wait for slow, deep pleasure that lasted a long time.

She smiled at his creativity. The shower, the bistro table, her computer desk, the deck, the sofa—everywhere in the house was a potential area for play.

It wasn't just sex either. They discussed their favorite books and movies, discovering how many they had in common. Conversations ranged from light to heavy, everything from food to politics. They occasionally cooked together. He took care of a bunch of house repairs and made plans for more. She cleaned and did the laundry. Work for both of them was on the extreme side, but somehow they carved out time to just be together.

The front bell rang, and she turned to see Hugo enter.

"What's up, sis?" He grinned and waved. "Got any whoopie pies?"

"Just for you, bro. Want a coffee with that?"

"Yup. Can you make a heart on top?"

"Absolutely." She turned to the counter to make his favorite caramel latte. "Have you talked to Mom and Dad lately?"

"Mom calls me every day," he groused. "Asks me if I'm eating okay. I tell her yes all the time, but I guess she doesn't believe me."

Jazz poured milk into the frothing pitcher. "It's nice to know she cares, right?"

Hugo huffed as he sat at a nearby table. "I guess it is. It's just that I have to tell her the same thing over and over and over and over again."

"Take it at face value, bro. There are some parents who don't give their children the time of day, let alone worry if they're eating and sleeping. Hold on while I finish this." The steamer hissed, drowning out any other noise.

As she poured the hot milk and drew a heart in the middle of the cup, the bell rang again. Jazz looked up, and her stomach dropped to the floor.

Four bikers entered the bakery. She didn't recognize them, but the logo on their cuts sent her into a tense panic. A fiery skull vomiting a stream of molten metal. They were part of the Slaggers. Two of them carried baseball bats, and one had a tire iron. They fanned out in the store, and the two other patrons quickly packed up their computers and coffee and skedaddled, leaving Jazz and Hugo alone.

Welcome. What can I get you? We have fresh donuts. "Welcome, you donuts." *Oh shit!*

Thankfully, they ignored her. "Where's that motherfucker?"

Hugo's eyes rounded, and he licked his lips nervously. "What's going on, sis?"

Jazz shushed her brother. "I don't know who you're talking about."

The one closest to the counter fingered the row of white china cups on top. "We know you're the girl he's been fucking." He clicked his tongue. "Weird that someone like him would be into stick figures, but different strokes for different folks, right?"

Jazz swallowed. Every muscle in her body was at the ready to grab her brother and run, but the other Slaggers hemmed them in. She could dart through the kitchen door and out the back, but how would she get to Hugo? Obviously, they'd found out that she and Wolf were an item and he worked here from time to time. How much more had they learned about him?

"Jazzy?" Hugo's voice sounded scared.

She put a strained smile on her face and formed her words as carefully as she could. "He's not here, and I don't know when he'll be back. If you want some coffee and Danishes to go, I can get that for you. My treat."

"No, thanks. I just need to leave a message for him." He placed his arm on the counter and, with one hard swipe, sent the stacked cups crashing to the floor.

This must have been the signal the other three bikers were waiting for. They started swinging and systematically destroyed the glass display counters, the coffee machines, the furniture—anything and everything that could be broken.

Hugo screamed as he dropped to the floor and covered his ears. Jazz crouched and hurried to his side, covering her brother with her body and shuffling him as close to the wall as possible. Shards of china and glass flew through the air. Broken pastries followed. One man pitched a table through the front window. Another one pounded on the register until it popped open. He stuffed all the cash into his pockets before yanking it from the counter and throwing it to the ground to beat it to pieces.

It seemed to go on forever. Hugo screamed and screamed, curled into Jazz as she held him for dear life.

"Please stop it!" she yelled. "Wolf isn't here! This is Bill and Madge's place! You're hurting them!"

The leader of the quartet shrugged and spat on the floor. "I don't give a fuck. Whoever gets in my way is gonna get hurt. Tell that fucker Ramrod was here. The Knights give us what we want, we'll stay away. They don't? We'll be back with more than bats next time."

Next time?

As they left, one of them yanked down the brass bell over the door. It clanged harshly once, and then there was silence save for Hugo's scared wails.

He was hyperventilating and in full panic mode. Jazz wanted to go that route herself, but she crammed that urge back into its box and calmed her brother. She rocked him back and forth, holding his body against her tightly. "They're gone, Hugo. They're gone, sweetheart."

It took several more minutes of gentle tones to get Hugo to reduce his hysterical crying to subdued sniffles.

"Why did they do that?" He wiped his nose on his sleeve as he released his death grip on her neck.

"I don't know, bro."

"They were so mean!"

"I know, I know."

Her mind combed through every response she could have. Collapsing into a blubbering heap was not an option. She needed to call someone. Police. Hugo's counselor. Wolf. Madge. Not necessarily in that order.

A passerby appeared at the broken window. "Oh my gawd, yinz okay? I'll call the police."

One task down. With trembling hands, Jazz pulled out her phone and dialed Wolf.

25

Wolf sat at one of the two round tables in the club. The Knights didn't have a formal meeting room, and he wasn't happy to be having this one in public. Thankfully, there were no dancers this time of the morning, so no one else was in the bar save the Iron City Knights.

There weren't words in the English language to describe the emotions from yesterday. When Jazz called him to say a group of Slaggers had come and trashed the bakery, the fury that erupted in his gut had no limit. He'd broken several traffic laws on his way to get to her. He found her sitting on the side-walk outside the ruined building with a swarm of flashing blue lights surrounding her. Hugo was clinging to her like a limpet and unwilling to let her go.

He didn't see any bullet holes, but there were several streaks of blood on her face and shoulders where glass had caught her. Hugo had a small cut over his left eye. Wolf guessed she had used her body to shield her brother from flying debris. She raised her eyes to meet his, and her expression was one he hoped he never had to see again.

He was ready to kill someone. Slowly. With a lot of pain.

That anger had not dissipated.

"This shit is going to stop. One way or another," he seethed.

Scrap sighed and scratched his scraggly beard. "I don't see what your woman's bakery has to do with us."

Wolf was incredulous at the club president's blasé attitude. "What the fuck do you mean, you don't see? Those fuckers named me. Named this club. They scared the shit out of my woman and told her they planned to come back with worse. Not even a blind man would mistake this shit!"

Scrap growled back, "The bakery is not our problem. No need for us to do anything."

"Are you fucking kidding me?" This came from

Quillon, normally the chillest guy in the club. He was regarding Scrap with disbelief. "The drive-by and the vape shop? We should have already taken the bull by the horns and finished this business then. It's gonna be harder to do that now."

"Did you fucking hear what I said? The bakery is not our problem!"

"So, we just hang Bill 'n' Madge out to dry?" Camshaft added his voice to the mix. "They torched the hippie's place and him with it. They extorted the auto parts place and the laundromat next to it. Marcie at the deli said they came to get money from her, too, and now they've destroyed the bakery where we've been getting our coffee for years. How much more is it gonna take before we do something?"

Scrap banged a heavy beer glass on the table in lieu of a gavel. "We don't have the men."

Wolf kept a tight lid on his anger. If he let it go, there's no telling what would come out. "We have three new recruits ready for patchover."

"We don't have enough weapons."

"How many do we need? Everyone here is armed. What the fuck are you waiting for?"

"I told you to leave it alone!" Scrap's roar stopped the conversation, but Wolf wasn't done.

This was it. Showtime. If there was going to be a

future for the Iron City Knights MC, someone needed to step up and lead it. In the next twenty minutes, the club would change or he would no longer be a part of it. "We cannot sit on the sidelines while our people are in danger. Scrap, if you can't see that, you need to step down."

Wolf was ready for a fight, but Scrap's next statement caught him off guard. "You're right. I'm old, and I'm tired. I don't have the same energy I used to, but this ain't no walk in the park. Decisions either keep us breathing or could get us dead. Anyone got the balls for this shit, have at it. Who's it gonna be?"

Baghouse and Melter both shook their heads and grumbled, "Not me," under their collective breaths. This was good, as they were Scrap's contemporaries and didn't have leadership qualities. The rest of the club stayed silent, waiting to see who spoke up first.

Scrap continued. "I thought so. When someone has the guts to take a bullet for a brother, then we'll talk. Until then, we'll keep a low profile."

Some muttering undertones came from the members as they turned away from the tables and went about any business they could find.

Wolf's temper relaxed as he reasoned out his response. Yeah, he could explode and make this meeting into a bigger shit show, or he could strategize and come up with a better solution.

He turned to Quillon with a raised brow. "Want a shot at it, brother?"

Quillon blew out a breath. "I've wondered about it, but I'm not the leader we need. I think you're the guy for it, Wolf. We need a restructuring with a solid core statement of who we are, where we came from, and what we're becoming. That's what you do best. That said, I agree with you about the Slaggers. We need to do something before someone else gets hurt or dead. I also agree with Scrap. We don't have the arms or the funds to go for a long war. My first suggestion is we find out how to get the tools we need to take on this fight, then plan our strategy."

Wolf nodded. "We need to get on that now, with or without Scrap. Do me a favor and put some of your gray matter to work. I don't want to wait until someone bleeds for us to get off our asses."

THE HOUSE WAS QUIET WHEN WOLF GOT HOME. Camshaft was on duty, which was a good thing because there was no way he'd leave Jazz by herself tonight. He found her at her computer desk, talking to some internet dude over a microphone that modi-fied her voice into something else.

"So, do I press Enter now?" Her tone was singsongy and high like a goofy college girl. "When do I press it?"

A heavily accented man's voice came back frustrated as hell. "No, no, no, no! Do not press Enter!"

"Whoops, I did it. Sah-ree! My bad. Goodness gracious, I never thought payin' my cousin's bail over the phone was this complicated. What jail is he in?"

"He was caught in the city of New Jersey."

Jazz pursed her lips as her hands moved. "The city of New Jersey? I thought New Jersey was a state."

"Don't you know your own country, ma'am?"

Wolf smiled as she cast her eyes to the ceiling, her mouth puckered in a thinking manner, and tapped the side of her face. She was so totally in character, and it was fun to watch. "I never was very good at geography. Which cousin is this again? I have a lot of them, and you know, some of them I don't care enough about to post a bond. What's his name?"

"How should I know his name? He's your cousin. What kind of idiot are you?"

"Uh, rude!" She swiped her hand and snapped her fingers in the air.

Wolf had to cover his mouth to keep from

laughing at her. She spotted him and grinned. "My boyfriend is here. I think I'm just gonna leave my cousin in jail. He needs to atone for all his sins and everything." Her fingers rapid-fired over the keyboard, and Wolf watched in fascination at the running screens.

"But, ma'am, your relative needs you to post this bond or else he will stay in jail for many nights."

"Not my problem, dude." She pressed Enter again and clapped her hands in delight. "Check your screen, Sparky."

"How? Where?"

"You're a fucking thief, and you're done. I reversed your money transactions, dude. Everything you took from people in the last few days has been returned. Find another way to make a living. If I catch you again, I'll break you into pieces so small, you'll never be able to touch a computer again."

The foreign curses cut off abruptly as she hung up. "I fried his computer. He won't be taking anyone's money again for a while." She sighed as she leaned back in her computer chair and rubbed her eyes with her fists. Her character disappeared, and all that was left was a tired woman. "It seems the more we shut down, the more pop up to take their place. Email scams, phone scams, text scams, phishing, and every day a new one. It makes me feel useless, like I'm trying to bail out the ocean with a teaspoon."

Wolf reached for her hands and drew her out of the chair. "You're not useless, babe. It might not seem that way to you, but think for a minute how many people you've helped and how many people you've saved. Delia would be in a world of hurt if you hadn't interfered. She's just one of many." He folded her in his arms. "You can't save them all, but you take care of the ones you can. Did you talk to Hugo today?"

She wrapped herself around him, hugging him close. "I called him earlier. He's still pretty shook up, but he worked his shift. Madge and Bill had the insurance adjuster come over today. Madge is thinking about giving the bakery up if they get a good settlement, so there's that."

He tucked her head into the spot between his shoulder and chest and gave a long sigh. It hadn't gotten old yet, the sensation of her body fitting against his so perfectly. He marveled for the four-hundred-thousandth time how well they meshed on multiple levels. "We'll see that they come out on top."

He loved that they had the same core values, work ethics, and common interests. Her generous nature matched his needs, and his did the same for her. Sex with Jazz was over-the-top good. It was the most genuine intimacy he'd ever experienced. When she gave herself to him, it was all of her. Nothing held back. He'd exposed the deepest parts of himself to her, and she accepted it without question. It made him love her even more.

Love. Yes, it was time he admitted it. He loved her. This beautiful, quirky, smart, talented woman had become the most important person in his life.

He leaned down and took her mouth softly. She molded her lips to his, opening up to his questing tongue and letting him in. He tasted sweet cherry from the hard candies she kept on her desk.

Yes, he loved Jasmine Hickling. Every last part of her.

He whispered against her lips. "I need to be inside you, babe. Right now. Can you take me?"

"Always," she whispered back.

They left a trail of clothes on the way to the bedroom. She lay back on the mattress, and he entered her immediately, plunging deep into her wetness. His movements started slow, then became more frantic, as if he needed to feel all of her at once. He came apart in her arms, filling her with himself until he couldn't tell where he ended and she began.

They lay in the bed, Wolf on his back and Jazz curled into his side and over him. His fingers stroked up and down her side, massaging and lightly squeezing her supple skin. Freya was sleeping in her basket near the open window. Cool breezes from the river wafted through the room, bringing freshness along with the city lights. Somewhere, a barge's horn sounded as it made its way across the water. All was well—at least at that moment.

"What happened at your meeting?" Jazz asked as she nuzzled into Wolf's side. "Are you allowed to tell me, or is it a big biker secret?"

"We used to have rules, but no one pays attention to them. That's the big problem with the club now. Too many workers and no leaders. That has to change." Her head rose and lowered as he took a big breath and let out a huge sigh. "Quillon and I have talked a lot about it, and someone needs to step up. The only ones that make sense are either him or me."

Her hand came to his abdomen, and she ran her finger over the feathers of his tattoo. "Do you want to be the president?"

"Honestly, no, but I might not have a choice. The Slaggers need to be taken down before someone else gets hurt or worse. When I think of what could have happened to you or Hugo? Fuck me, I want to kill someone."

She paused in her tracings. "Wouldn't that get the club into trouble?"

"Potentially, but I can't see a way out of it. The Slaggers were allowed to run rampant for so long that they're out of control. It's gonna take some serious firepower to knock them down." He jammed a hand over his face. "They have us outmanned and outgunned, even with the new people our ally sent us. Scrap has his head buried so deep he won't deal with it." He let out a heavy breath. "If we don't do anything, more people like Bill and Madge are going to suffer. If we step in, the club will face bloodshed and probably have to fight the police too. Denny has been a friend of ours for a long time, but he'd have no choice but to arrest one or more of us if we go to war and bullets start flying." He stared at the ceiling and huffed a short laugh. "Christ on a cracker, it doesn't matter how we handle this, it's lose-lose."

Jazz's fingers pulled at his nipple piercing as she listened to him. When he'd finished, she was quiet for a few moments, then said, "Just a suggestion, but there are other ways to deal with this besides guns and bullets."

He ran his fingers over her hair, gently lifting and smoothing the colored strands. "I'm all ears, babe."

She cleared her throat. "No matter what, everyone has to have an income and a way to get to it. If they're into extortion and other illegal shit, they have to have a place to clean their money. It shouldn't be hard to find it and mess it up."

He shook his head, unwilling to even consider it. "I'm not putting you in the line of fire, babe."

"They would never know it was me. I can get in and out without them finding me. Without their finances, they'd be crippled. I can leave an obvious breadcrumb trail for the cyber police to find. Easy peasy lemon squeezy."

"I don't want you involved in this. It's too dangerous. These people are not joking."

"I'm not either."

He shifted to place her on her back while he hovered over her. "I will not risk losing you, Jazz. Stay out of it."

She stared up at him, and the tears forming in her eyes nearly undid him. "They already hurt my family. Bill and Madge. Hugo. Please don't ask me to sit back and watch them hurt you, too, when I have the ability and power to do something about it."

Wolf heard the earnestness in her voice. He could

argue his fear more, but he recognized her need to help protect her people, and that included him. "I need to wrap my head around this idea and talk to Quillon and the boys. Can you hold off for a bit?"

"Yes, I can hold off for a bit."

He leaned down and kissed her. "I love you." The simple words weren't enough to describe what he had in his heart and mind, but they were all he had. "I love you so fucking much, Jazz. I'd go crazy if something happened to you."

"Okay," she responded, her voice a bit quavery.

He squeezed her. "You gonna say it back?"

"I love you too?"

"Babe, now's not the time to ask a question."

She smiled. "I love you too."

26

Candie cried out as the man rammed himself inside her from behind. "Yeah, baby, do me hard. Do me harder than all those fuckers."

He obliged by pounding into her body mercilessly as she bent over at the waist and grabbed the cheap footboard of the motel bed. She liked him taking her this way, and the rougher the better. It hurt, but she wanted it to hurt. Wanted it to tear her up so she could feel something that matched her anger.

"More!"

"What's got you so upset, *priya*?" the handsome man teased as he gripped her hips hard enough to leave bruises.

"That fuckin' jagoff Wolf. Thinks he can get away

with firing me. Well, he and his cunt girlfriend got another thing coming!"

Someday she needed to find out this guy's name. He called himself Enforcer, and she guessed it was a road name from some other MC. She didn't give a shit as long as he had money and a big dick that stayed hard for a long time. He was handsome as hell, even with that scar near his left ear.

"How dare they fire me! I'm the star of the gawd-damn show," she said as she repositioned her arms to brace against the violent pounding.

"Are they always together?"

"How the fuck should I know? If he's not at her place, he's at the club. If he's not there, then he's at that fucking bakery. I can't believe he's fucking a skinny blue-haired coffee nerd!" No matter. She'd get them back somehow. "Aren't you supposed to be fucking me?"

His answer was to wrap a scarf around her neck and pull back, choking her as he continued to thrust. She vaguely heard him talking but didn't understand the words. Probably cursing her and calling her a whore. She smiled.

This was the second time she'd met him and the first time she'd fucked him. He wasn't a Slagger, but he hung out at their clubhouse, so maybe he was one of those wannabe bikers or a new prospect looking to join. After Wolf fired her, she immediately ran to the Slagger compound and told them all the dirt she could think of about the Knights. Especially Wolf and his fucking cunt girlfriend. When she saw this dude was there, she walked up to him and asked point-blank if he wanted to fuck. They drove straight to the place she brought her clients, and he rented the room. Not thirty seconds after they entered, she was bent over taking it from him. No foreplay. No lube. No talking. Just raw animal fucking. Perfect for the mood she was in.

"Where's her place?"

He yanked her back, slamming himself inside her, making their skin clap together. Candie's knees nearly buckled.

"Camshaft said it was some old house in a dip near the greenway. He helped Wolf do some home improvement shit. Wolf and his cunt playing house together! Makes me fucking sick." A thought occurred to her. "Why the fuck do you want to know?"

"Maybe I'll go kill them both for you."

His thrusts became more violent, and Candie felt the first smidgeon of fear. For all the violent thrusting, he sounded completely in control. Fuck that!

Orgasm was just at the horizon. She coughed once as the scarf tightened. "Is that all you got?"

He ripped out of her pussy, lined up with her ass, and plunged inside. The pain made her scream and come at the same time. "That's it! Fuck me! Fuck my ass!"

The scarf tightened again.

27

Jazz flexed her fingers. This wasn't going to be as easy, but what choice did she have? The Slaggers had already trashed Bill and Madge's place to the point of ruin and terrorized her brother.

What would happen when they came after Wolf with guns blazing?

This was going to end, just not in a big bloody shootout on the streets of Pittsburgh. It would piss Wolf off like crazy when he found out about her interference, but if her hacking capabilities kept him and her other loved ones safe, then she would willingly risk his wrath.

Jazz opened her programs and logged into the dark web. Her hands skimmed over the keys as she searched for the sites she needed while keeping her presence hidden. First rule of a hacker and a scam-shielder? Find the money trail. Everyone needed to launder it.

It took some time traipsing through information as related to the Slaggers, but the sniffer program she designed found the first part of what she wanted. Huge amounts of money flowed from a mom-and-pop dry-cleaning service near the Slaggers MC compound. The profits from this little business tripled several years ago, which she thought should have set off an alarm with the state, but as long as taxes were paid on time, no one paid attention to the oddity. A little research drummed up information that the owners had been deceased for seven years. That certainly was at odds with a business that was thriving. Google street maps showed the front of the building locked up solid with a Closed sign on the front window that was so old it was peeling away. If any dry-cleaning was taking place, it was very little. The new owner was none other than James Higgenbotham, aka Ramrod of the Slaggers MC, and it appeared that they had just under a million in the business. More like drug trade revenues and extortion fees.

No wonder they had such firepower.

Jazz ran a reconciliation program and flagged several bank accounts that would trigger audits. She debated on inserting her special virus but decided corrupting this program wouldn't be enough. Tapping the keys, she systematically transferred money and deleted those accounts, leaving no trace of herself but dropping a few pins that looped back and framed James as the initiator of these transactions. She scattered the money as donations to dozens of different charities around the country: a children's home in Nebraska, a women's shelter in Idaho, a high school marching band in Oklahoma. Simple transfers that she set up as gifts from fictitious or anonymous donors. She thought about giving some money to Bark-Off Dog Treats, where her brother worked, but someone might notice a connection between the chief baker and the guy their club scared the shit out of recently. Once the money appeared in those accounts, she deleted all transaction histories and erased any pathways that would lead back to her or the Knights.

Then she planted bugs in their system that would send out big red flags to cyber authorities to not only cripple their drug network but also give access to the DEA, wrapping them up like a Christmas gift with a big shiny bow. She didn't have to do much more than lay a wide trail of data breadcrumbs and the Slaggers would be toast.

Jazz imagined it would only be a matter of hours before they figured out their money was gone. If anyone in the Slaggers MC had some computer skills, they might be able to trace the dummy accounts, but they would all lead to James. Any other suspicions would drop when they found out the money had vanished.

Freya jumped on her lap and butted her head against Jazz's chin.

"Yeah, just give it a little time. Our friendly neighborhood Ramrod is going to be in a world of hurt soon. He'll be lucky if his own gang doesn't get him before the police do."

Something else bothered her about this mess. The Slaggers were pretty much done after everything played through, but what was the bigger picture behind them? If she expanded the margins, was there more to find?

Jazz took a breath and reminded herself that she was sitting in her own house, in front of her own computer with Freya purring away on her lap. She was well hidden to the point of being virtually invisible on the net. Still, fear crept into her brain as she dove deep into the dark unknown.

What she found terrified her.

Data poured over the screen. Dates and times of deliveries, routes and modes of transportation, countries of origin and of receiving, distribution centers, and more. The longer she explored this network, the more information she found about this gigantic intricate web. Even worse was the contents. Whoever owned this massive machine dealt with more than just drugs. Arms deals appeared, and they apparently sold to both opposing sides. The main financing for this operation? A plethora of large-scale call centers that kept the money flowing.

"Holy shit!" she said aloud, and Freya stopped her purring and opened one yellow eye for a moment to glare at her. Whoever was in charge of this network had some serious computer skills.

Tears came to Jazz's eyes. She dashed them away as she noted that she'd been at this cyber deep dive for close to four hours. She thought about releasing her custom virus and letting it wreak havoc on this system, but she remembered Copperpot's warning about potential ramifications.

This was too big for her to take on by herself. Maybe even too big for all the scam-shielders if they tried together. Should this go to the FBI? CIA? Interpol?

As much as she wished she could do something now, she needed answers. She tagged the site, then deleted and erased any trace of her existence in that network. As she exited, she saw a list of IP addresses and recognized one of them. The remnants of the giant scammer site she took down was in this network, and someone was rebuilding it.

She had to talk to Copperpot.

Once out of the dark web, she tried to contact the mentor and friend she had never met. Usually he would answer quickly. This time, he was silent.

A sick sensation bloomed in her belly. Something was wrong.

28

The strip club was wild tonight. Almost frantic. Perhaps it was just the antsy buzz that sat in Wolf's gut like a lead weight. A few patrons had asked about Candie, but so far no one had complained. The newest girl, Sheila, made up for the missing headliner, and the enthusiasm showed in the collection of green bills hanging in a row from her G-string.

Quillon was there for a change, mostly because the two of them had to show a united front to the other club members—and, if needed, to the Slaggers. They stood close to the front door, continuously scanning the crowd for trouble.

"My gut says something's about to go down, but I can't put my finger on it." Quillon had a knack for reading people. So far, nothing had sent up alarms, but his words belied his easy demeanor.

"I'm getting the same vibe, brother. Shit is about to hit the fan, and I wish I knew who was throwing it or which direction it'll come from."

Quillon grunted and nodded at Camshaft, who'd stationed himself on the other side. "Any blowback from the Candie thing?"

"Nothing so far. Kinda strange. I expected her to come blustering in by now and offer to blow Scrap to get her job back."

"She might as well suck off a stone statue. Scrap has nothing to do with women. Any woman."

"Why is that?"

Quillon scratched his chin. "Wife left him before his accident. Rumor is, she took off for some guy she met online. Baghouse said she tried to come back once, and Scrap threw her out. Said she ended up in Florida of all places. He won't talk about it or speak her name. You already know Scrap is one of the bitterest human beings on this planet. He cares for no one, and that's getting more and more apparent by how he treats this club."

Wolf glanced over the row of men and thought about Quillon's insight. It explained a lot, but it was no excuse for the half-hearted leadership. He was convinced they were on the right path in seeking a new president. Part of him wanted Quillon to fill that role. The other part wanted to do it himself.

"I know what you're thinking, brother," Quillon stated. "Let me tell you straight, I do not have the time nor the energy to turn this club around. I can help, but I can't lead. We've been talking a lot, and I had a personal conversation with Scrap. We'll take a formal vote soon, but for all intents and purposes, you're in the hot seat now. You tell me what you need from me and you'll have it."

An invisible weight landed on Wolf's shoulders. The responsibility of leading and rebuilding this club intimidated him, but someone had to step up. He guessed that someone was him.

"Through the fires of hell, men of steel are forged."

Time to ignite the furnace.

Sheila finished her set and bounced off the stage, her fake double-D's having a party all to themselves. Wolf grinned in amusement as he saw Camshaft shift his junk from one side of his jeans to the other. The younger man had always been vigilant when he came to his security job, but it was a nice distraction to see his human reaction to a great pair of tits.

Yeah, they were nice, but he preferred the natural movement of Jazz's breasts.

The night wore on, but Wolf's gut instincts never waned. His muscles grew sore from the constant ready tension, and his head started buzzing with an impending headache. He thought about texting Jazz to see if she could bring him a migraine injection but decided against it. Her sleep patterns were just as irregular as his, so she should be in bed getting some shut-eye. At least he hoped she was. He didn't remember her saying she would hold off on the hacking thing.

Quillon raised a concerned eyebrow at Wolf's muttered curse. "What's on your mind?"

"I should have made her promise me."

Quillon grunted. "I have no idea what you're talking about, but if it's over a woman, I'm glad you found someone. I never thought I'd get Tracie, but we're coming up on our anniversary. Best thing I've ever done is put a ring on her finger."

Wolf nodded. "That's in the plans."

Crossman appeared before them, nervous as hell. "Yinz gotta come out now. Denny is here. Somethin' happened over at the motel, and you're not gonna like it."

Wolf and Quillon exchanged glances before moving as a unit to the front door.

Officer Denny was standing outside, along with

four other policemen in full uniform. The man's face showed his age with every year of hard living from his chosen profession. "Evenin', Wolf. I gotta ask you a couple questions." He sighed, and his mouth turned down farther. "Where were you earlier tonight?"

"I was at home with my girl, then ran by the bakery to check on things before coming to work."

Denny shook his head. "Shit. What time frame was that?"

Wolf's senses shot to high alert. "I left Jazz around seven thirty and got here around nine thirty."

"Did you go by the motel?"

Wolf didn't have to ask which motel Denny referred to. "No. What's going on?"

"When was the last time you saw Candie Sweet? I understand you two had a fight when you fired her. Was it a lovers' quarrel?"

"Candie was fired because she broke too many rules too many times. We haven't been lovers in years. Did something happen to her?"

Denny let out a breath. "Yeah, something happened. We got an anonymous tip that someone heard screams coming from that place, and not the good-time kind. We found your former stripper lying face down with a scarf around her neck. She'd been torn up pretty bad and strangled to death. The caller told us he saw you leave her room. Named you specifically as the one who killed her. We have to do a more thorough investigation, but until we get more evidence, I got no choice." He shook his head. "You have no clue how much I hate doin' this. Wolf, I'm afraid you're under arrest for the murder of Candie Sweet."

29

JAZZ GRITTED HER TEETH AT LIZ'S ASSUMPTIVE statement. No, she didn't have kids at home, but she didn't sit on her ass with nothing to do but watch hours of TV either. When Liz called for some babysitting help, Jazz hadn't expected her sister to show up at her house with all three kids in tow. Originally, Jazz was going to head over to the Comers' house to sit with Bill so Madge got a break. It was becoming more and more obvious that the man wouldn't recover much of his mobility. His health was in a permanent state of limbo, and the two bakery owners showed serious signs of depression. Anytime Jazz could visit their home and give Madge a little time to herself was a big help. Truthfully, she also needed a break from her own head, as she'd spent a lot of hours thinking about what she'd discovered on the dark web. Tonight's plans had changed with Liz and her kids.

The family appeared at her door with no warning around seven. Liz was dressed to the nines with full makeup and her hair styled and sprayed for a night out. It only took half a heartbeat for Jazz to realize her sister was on the prowl for a new man. Preferably one with money this time. It was now past eleven, and the texts Jazz sent for an ETA had gone unanswered until this one.

Jazz: It wasn't a problem earlier, but don't they need to go home and get to bed?

Liz: They can spend the night with you.

Jazz's mouth dropped open. It had not been on her radar that her nephews would crash at her place. What about when Wolf came home?

> Jazz: Where am I supposed to put them? I don't have an extra bedroom or bed. Not even sleeping bags.

> Liz: They'll be fine for one night with blankets on the floor.

Exasperation colored Jazz's mind. Surely her sister wasn't serious.

> Jazz: Liz, this isn't acceptable!

It took a minute before the dots bounced around.

> Liz: For fuck's sake I'm taking the night off! Unless one of them is bleeding, don't bother me!

Jazz stared at the words. She got it. Parents were still human and sometimes needed space from their kids. Liz worked about twenty hours a week at the corner convenience store, and preschool plus day care was super expensive for three kids. She was with the boys almost all the time. Leo paid child support but hadn't stepped up to do anything else in weeks. Ian, Ivan, and Isaac spent more time with their grandparents than their father.

"Looks like we're going to have a pajama party,"

she told them as she pulled up Wolf's number and fired off a quick text about the boys being at the house.

> Jazz: My nephews are spending the night. Careful of little bodies on the floor when you come home.

The dots didn't move. That was odd, as Wolf usually answered within seconds. Jazz slipped the phone into her back pocket and turned to the task of finding enough bedding. "All right, munchkins, let's see what we can build."

"I'm hungry!" The declaration came from Ian as he jumped and executed a front flip from the couch to the floor, making the whole house rattle.

Ivan chased Freya into the bedroom and yelled, "Me too!"

Jazz put a hand to her head. She had little kid food other than cereal. "Umm, it's pretty late. Shouldn't you guys be in bed already?"

Ian paused. "Mama doesn't make us go to bed. We stay up as late as we want."

Jazz blinked. "How do you get enough sleep?"

The boy didn't answer. He climbed on the back of the couch to flip himself again, this time knocking over a model of a Klingon warship. Jazz cringed as the fragile neck snapped and the round bridge compartment rolled under the couch.

Maybe food would be a good distraction. "I have Cheerios. Would that be okay?"

"I want pizza!"

"Yeah! Pizza!"

Jazz watched as Ian started stomping around in a circle, punctuating each syllable. Ivan joined him. Isaac woke up and started crying. No wonder Liz needed a break from this chaos. Then again, a lot of it was her own making.

Jazz shook her head. No, she wasn't a parent, but it seemed like the boys should be on a more routine schedule and would benefit from a little discipline.

She opened her phone and typed in an order at her favorite delivery place that was still open. "Pepperoni?"

"I want cheesy sticks too!"

"Yeah, cheesy sticks!"

Isaac's cries increased. Jazzy fired off an order on the app, then hurried over to pick the baby up from the porta-pen. One whiff told her what the problem was. "Whoa, that's a serious-smelling fart blossom, kid."

There was no place to change the baby but on her bed. Jazz didn't want to leave the other boys alone in fear of her furniture surviving their energetic play, but the wails weren't stopping until that dirty diaper was gone. "Yinz need to calm down for bit. Pizza is on the way. I'm gonna change the baby, then after you eat, it's bedtime."

Ivan paused and cocked his head to the side. "How are we supposed to go to bed when we don't have any here?"

"We'll build a blanket fort. There's a card table in the closet. Thinks you guys can pull it out?"

The pizza mantra changed to a blanket fort chant as the two rug rats ran to take care of the task.

That will keep them busy for a little while.

Isaac chortled and put a grin on his face once the messy diaper came off his bottom. Jazz tried not to gag at the amount of shit that came from that little body. Even his clothes were covered. "Not a fart blossom. More like an Old Faithful gusher."

Isaac cooed and grabbed at his toes. Jazz used half a box of wipes to get the small body clean. Since there wasn't a change of clothes, she grabbed one of her smallest T-shirts just as something crashed in the other room.

Are you guys okay? What happened? Anyone hurt? "Hurt okay?"

"Auntie J? How much did those big glasses with the phone booth on them cost?"

Jazzy closed her eyes and gave a moment of silence for her collector Tardis beer mugs. "Don't touch the glass. I'll clean it up when I'm—"

An arc of pee sprayed across her chest, surprising her with its warmth. Jazz looked down at the gurgling baby. "Proud of yourself, aren't you?"

She swiftly diapered and clothed Isaac. She was about to change her shirt when another crash filled the air, this time followed by a wail.

"Auntie J? Ivan broke your bookcase."

Jazz hurried into the room and placed the baby in the porta-pen. Ivan sat crying and holding his head. "Are you hurt? What's wrong?"

Ian swung the custom Harry Potter wand around. "He wanted to see the dragon on the really high shelf and tried to climb up. It didn't work."

No shit. Irritation crept up her spine, and she had to stifle herself from losing her temper. "Please stop climbing, jumping, running, or any other physical activity in the house."

Ian answered her by somersaulting into a table and almost landing in the pile of glass shards.

Jazz clenched her jaw and fists. She stood in her main living area with her shattered Tardis collection on the floor with her books, the wall shelves broken, one kid crying like a banshee, another one oblivious to his own destruction, a baby who just peed all over her, and her boyfriend hadn't texted back yet.

Could the night get worse?

Apparently so.

The bell rang.

Ivan forgot about his hurt head and yelled, "Pizza!" Both boys barreled to the door and yanked it open.

Yes indeed, a pizza deliveryman was there.

Along with two large men in biker cuts she'd never seen before. One was completely bald with some serious tattoos, and the other was an earthly version of a Viking god. The pizza guy stood between the two of them with a square box in his hand, staring up with round wide eyes at the giants surrounding him.

"Um... pizza delivery for Jazz?"

JAZZ CAME INTO THE LIVING AREA, FRESH FROM the shower with clean clothes and damp hair. Amazingly, the boys were calmly playing a boardgame with Table, and Stud was crumpling the empty pizza box into a shape that would fit in the trash can. The glass had been cleaned up, and her books were stacked neatly next to the broken shelf.

Two random men—correction, two random bikers showing up at her door in the middle of the night wasn't normal. The Viking introduced himself as Stud of the Dragon Runners MC, and the bald man was Table. He said a friend of theirs called Bruiser sent them.

"You'll know him as Copperpot."

Earlier, Table took one look at the out-of-control boys and stepped in. He pointed to the couch and said, "Sit." He didn't yell or say the word with a mean, nasty tone, but there was a definite alpha vibe to him. The screaming children stopped and stared for half a beat before plopping themselves down and remaining silent. Jazz vacillated between amazement and envy at the man's control.

Now, the kids were fed and finally winding down. Isaac was curled up in the porta-pen, already out for the night. Ivan rubbed sleepily at his eyes.

Table placed his hands on his knees and stood up. "Where do I put them?"

Jazz sniffed. "I guess they can go in my bed together, and I'll take the couch." Wolf still hadn't answered her texts, and she was worried about that.

"I'll deal with everything when my...." *What should I call him? Boyfriend? Lover? Dude?* "Boy-ver dudefriend." *Seriously, Jazz?* She shook her hands in the air. "I'm sorry. I have a lot going on right now."

Stud and Table exchanged glances. The blond man sighed as he spoke. "Yeah, we got that part. We're not trying to add to your burden, but there's something you need to know. Let's go sit for a bit and talk."

All three settled in the living room. The two large men dwarfed her couch, and she perched on the only other chair in the room. "So, what do you need to tell me?"

Stud leaned forward, his elbows on his knees, and his handsome face grew serious. "Our brother, Bruiser, sent us up here to warn you. He got targeted and almost killed because of the computer shit he does. No one in the Dragon Runners MC knew about his cyber-vigilante side game, but apparently he and a bunch of your other scam-shielder group pissed someone off. Big-time."

Jazz's hands began to shake. "Oh no! Is... is Copperpot... uh... Bruiser okay?"

Table spoke this time. "Yeah, he's okay. He's got his cabin fixed up tighter than Fort Knox. He was able to call out before he took a bullet. The best we can figure is the attempt was supposed to look like a night hunting accident. We got him to the hospital in time. It was serious, but he's okay. He told us all about this shit with his scam-shielder group and how people are winding up dead. He believes it's just one guy, a hired assassin to take out all the shielders. He won't say why, but it doesn't matter. What matters is keeping everyone else safe."

Jazz's heart clenched in pain. "So, the reason I don't see Glyndathegood or Bomber or Muscleman online is that they're... gone?"

Stud sighed again, his lips set in a grim line. "I'm so sorry to be the one bearing this news."

Guilt flooded her senses and took all her focus. "It's all my fault. If I hadn't gotten so cocky and shut down that stupid call center—" Tears filled her eyes, and a sob prevented her from saying more.

Stud took her hands and forced her to look at him. "Hey, that's enough. Do not blame yourself for whatever is happening. Bruiser gave us a few details about how he and his group target scammer scum-bags. *They* are the criminals, not you."

"But—"

"No buts. None of this is on you. Got it?"

The man could say that on repeat dozens of times and she would still feel responsible. The tears tracked down her face, and she let them fall. "All I ever wanted to do was help people. I get so mad when I hear about someone getting ripped off. Madge and Bill, they worked so hard, and now their business is gone and their insurance might not be enough and—"

She found herself enfolded in a set of strong arms. Her forehead pushed against a leather cut, and she sobbed into it.

"It's a lot to take in. We get it. We're not pointing fingers, sweetheart. We're not even mad about Bruiser. Who we're mad at are the bad guys. You're not one of the bad guys. All we want to do now is help you protect yourself and your family."

"Cool. Let's start with you taking your fucking hands off my woman," Wolf snarled as he suddenly appeared in the doorway.

30

THE SUMMER HEAT IN WASHINGTON, DC, didn't stop the hordes of tourists who flocked to the National Mall. Crowds of people walked from the National Air and Space Museum across to the National Art Gallery in a never-ending flow. The Capitol Building sat at one end with its majestic domed spire within sight of the Washington Monument and the Lincoln Memorial farther down. Beyond the mall perimeter sat other buildings full of workers going about their daily business, including the Library of Congress and the J. Edgar Hoover Building, which held the headquarters of the FBI.

The man had no interest in the museums, art or history. His goal was the building just a few blocks north of the National Mall. The US National Central Bureau, otherwise known as Interpol.

Technically, he should go to a field office first, as the central agency was for law enforcement assistance, not for the general public. But he had the feeling he would be welcome inside once he showed someone what he had.

Nassar stood outside the building and stared at the security doors. Fatima and his children were in Pennsylvania, staying with a distant relative of hers. The escape from their own country into this one had been long and tedious. They'd started travel by train and then boat, hopping countries in a roundabout way through port areas that had less security until arriving in London and securing a flight to the United States. He'd tried to plan for any contingency, from tourist papers to whatever his children might inadvertently say to a stranger. Ironically, their money was all on Visa gift cards, so there were no banking records to track. They'd lived with new identities, fake passports, and the constant fear that something would tip off either his old employers or the authorities. Either way, he could get screwed for life or his family destroyed in the process.

He closed his eyes and sent up a prayer, hoping that when he walked into the building, he could walk out again. His hand shook as he pressed the button on the intercom.

"This is a restricted area. Please step away from the building," a disembodied voice announced. It could have been a man or a woman. What it wasn't was friendly.

Nassar wiped the sweat from his brow and licked his lips. "I have information to report about the network collapse a few months ago and international cybercrimes." He pulled out the flash drive he'd smuggled across the world. "Names. Dates. Transactions. All of them here."

He held his breath as he waited.

Then the door opened.

Nassar let out a long sigh, and his entire body went numb. He raised his chin and stepped through.

31

Wolf leaned his head back on the couch. He was uncomfortable as hell, but there was nowhere else to be. The boys had crashed in Jazz's bedroom, leaving the two of them to rough it in the living room. She was curled into his side and probably just as uneasy as he was.

First thing I'm gonna do when this blows over is either find a new place or expand this one.

Wolf had seen where the property lines lay, and there was room to build out some additions. His mind designed as he shifted to find a better position. Extend the foundation for an open great room with a cathedral ceiling. Knock out a wall in the current living room to make it a loft. Master bedroom suite on the other side leading to the deck facing the river.

Clear the land between the house and the street for a side yard and proper driveway. Two small bedrooms downstairs used for guests or office space or—

Let's not get too far ahead of ourselves.

He'd stayed at the station longer than he wanted to, but they had to let him go when his alibi checked out. Denny seemed relieved when he opened the cell door. Yeah, there was paperwork, but his cop friend would take care of it without a big fuss.

"I hope there aren't any bad feelings between us. Nothing connects you or anyone else to Candie's murder. We got shit for evidence, as in nothing. *Good for you, but bad for us. It's gonna be tough to solve this. We may never find out the truth."*

No witnesses. No hair, semen, or other physical evidence. No credit card or money trail. Whoever did Candie was a ghost.

The constant uneasiness in his gut amplified by a thousand after the conversation with the two visiting bikers.

"Bruiser said he's got his end covered. We don't know how, but we trust him to keep himself and us safe. Can we trust you to do the same for her?"

He hoped so. It seemed like the world had turned into the latest James Bond screenplay. A hired assassin? That was some seriously far-fetched fantasy shit that's only supposed to happen in books or movies.

He glanced down at the sleeping woman beside him. There were deep shadows underneath her eyes, and she'd lost weight she didn't need to lose. The world put a huge burden on her shoulders that she carried as best as she could. She was no Atlas, though. Wolf recalled the Greek myth of the Titan god condemned to hold up the sky for eternity. His mouth contracted. All those other people who'd been killed had been shut off from others and isolated. Even this guy, Bruiser, had hidden his shielder activities from his brothers. They would have to deal with that on their own.

"We trust him to keep himself and us safe. Can we trust you to do the same for her?"

That question had only one answer. It was tough and something he really didn't want to do, but there was very little choice in the matter.

He'd face the consequences later as long as his woman and her family stayed protected.

Carefully, he moved Jazz from underneath his arm and settled her back on the couch. He tossed a fleece blanket with a big purple nebula on it over her and waited to make sure she stayed asleep. Outside on the landing, he pulled out his phone and dialed

Camshaft. "I need you to come to my place and keep watch until I get back."

The sounds of pumping music came through the speaker. "We have a full house here, brother, but I can send Tugger over there."

Wolf didn't particularly want the newest recruit to guard his family, but he had little choice. Tugger was named after the winch at the mines that lifted heavy equipment from the earth's depths. The man wasn't the brightest bulb in the pack, but he was available, and Wolf didn't plan to be gone any longer than he had to. "Do it."

Wolf waited until the younger man showed up, then left the house and headed out on his bike, crossing over the bridge and into the city. People still roamed the streets at this hour, but he ignored them. His focus was on a different goal, one he never thought he'd have to take up again, but circumstances had come full circle, and he needed to step up.

Once he reached the storage facility, he had to scroll through his phone to find the notes on the combination code. The buttons beeped as he entered the numbers, and the gate rolled back. Three minutes later, he stood in front of the unit he'd rented years ago. He never understood why he didn't get rid of the contents a long time ago. Perhaps somewhere in his subconscious, he thought he'd have to open this part of his life again. He sighed and looked up the second code.

The air in the unit was musty and warm. There was a single bulb hanging from the ceiling, and he pulled the string to turn it on. Two sets of shelves graced the walls of the narrow space; each one held locked boxes of various sizes. With laser focus, Wolf moved between them and started opening and inspecting.

32

Jazz came awake when Freya jumped on her and buried her claws in her thighs. "Ugh, I got it, I got it. Breakfast is coming."

Her normally placid cat wasn't having it. Instead of the insistent meow, the cat screeched and slapped her several times in the face. The crazy behavior was enough to make Jazz fully wake up. "What the hell is wrong with you?"

The cat crouched on Jazz's chest, trembling and staring with wide eyes. Saliva dripped from her panting mouth, and she growled instead of purred.

That's when Jazz noticed the smell. Wood and chemical. Noxious. Smoky. Not like a campfire, but like—

Oh shit!

She sat up and gagged as she sucked in a lungful of smoke. It was thick, rising in a steady haze up the stairs from the bottom of the house. The floor under her feet radiated heat. What the hell was happening?

But her instincts already told her.

Shit! Dammit! Fuck!

Where is Wolf?

She exploded off the couch and screamed for the boys. "Ian! Ivan! Get out of the house!" She snatched Isaac from his crib and scooped up Freya.

Ian stumbled into the living space and started coughing. The smoke was getting thicker.

"What's that smell?" he mumbled.

"There's a fire. Move faster."

"I need shoes."

"I'll get them."

"I don't know where they are."

The fire alarm finally kicked in and let out a shrill scream. Jazz lost it. "I don't care about your shoes! Get out of the house! Now!"

She half dragged Ivan from the bed, but he didn't act out for once. Maybe it was the urgency in her voice that got the little boy to move, or the fact that the room was filling up with smoke. Jazz snagged her cell phone from her computer table as she pushed the two kids to the front door. She stopped short of stepping out and stared in horror at what she saw.

The walkway was gone. Pulled down or broken out so they couldn't cross it to the street. And there was no way to get out through the bottom floor.

They were stuck in a burning house.

She could see the flames clearly licking up both sides of the house. The bushes that rested against the walls were on fire, sending sparks into the air.

How did this happen?

Worry about that later, Jazz. Just get the boys to safety.

Ian started crying, and Ivan followed his brother's lead. They clung to Jazz as she stood trying to find a way out. The bridge was gone. Did she have anything that she could substitute? Planks from the bed? The closet door?

Short of leaping back and forth across the gap, she had nothing. Could she do that? Jump across carrying a child? She'd have to get a running start and do it several times. Hopefully, she'd make it each way without dropping anyone or missing the mark. The shrubs below had ignited and were flaring up. If she fell, it would be bad. Very bad.

She handed Freya to Ian, and the cat transferred her death grip to the crying little boy. Jazz forced her trembling hand to be still and swiped the screen on her phone.

"911, what's your emergency?"

Jazz could barely hear the operator over the boys' wailing and the dull roar of the burning bushes. *There's a fire! We're on the landing! Can't get out!* "We're on fire! Shit, I mean the house is on fire, and we're trapped!"

"What's your address?"

She rattled it off. Isaac added his protest to the cacophony. "Please hurry!"

Never before had she felt so helpless.

She huddled with the three boys on the remnants of the landing. Sparks from the fire underneath spit into the air around them as the house continued to burn. "It's okay. It's okay. Help is coming. We'll be fine." Tears flowed down her cheeks as she prayed she hadn't just lied to her panicking nephews. She hugged them close as they clung to her, still crying with fear.

"Jazz!" a voice yelled from the road. The smoke was thick, but she could make out a form. Wolf was there just across the broken bridge. "Hang on!"

A ladder slid across the span. The same one he'd used to get to her roof and replace some shingles earlier this month and had rested in the dip ever since. She moved slightly back into the house to allow it space to rest on the landing. A moment later, Wolf appeared, crawling across the makeshift connection.

"Listen up, boys. We're gonna play horsey, but one at a time. Ian, you're first. I want you to get on my back and hold as tight as you can. It's a short ride, and you can make it, yeah? Then Ivan, and you'll take care of him while I carry Isaac. Once we get across, Jazz, you'll follow. Can you do that, baby?"

"What about Freya?"

Wolf's eyes landed on the trembling animal. "Sorry, cat. I'll make it up to you later." He took the feline by the scruff and tossed her across the span to the road. The screech was akin to a kitty cussword, but she landed alive and indignant on the road. "All right, let's go."

Jazz held her breath as Wolf made the journey with Ian clinging like a monkey to his back. She did the same while watching him do it again with Ivan.

"How will you carry Isaac?" she coughed out. The acidic smoke was thicker now and was starting to choke her.

"I'll manage. As soon as you see me get to the other side, you come too. This place is ready to collapse on itself."

"Okay."

He held the baby with one arm to his chest and started across. His movements were slower, and Jazz's focus pinpointed on the man as if her sheer willpower alone would keep him from slipping. He made it to the road and turned to wave her over.

A thought occurred to her. "Just a second!" She turned and ran back into the house.

"Jazz! No!"

She ignored his shout and dropped to her hands and knees, scrambling to her computer desk. The goal was the external hard drive she used as a backup for all her data. If someone was out to get them, there might be evidence on here they would need. She shoved it in the waistband of her leggings and crawled to the open door.

Those few seconds were critical but costly. Her lungs seized up with smoke, and she couldn't get a clean breath. Coughing violently, she made it to the ladder and started across, feeling the rungs underneath with her hands and feet. It was harder than it looked. Only five or so feet, but it seemed like miles. She had to stop several times, her head spinning like a Tilt-A-Whirl ride as she forced her way forward.

"Come on, Auntie J, you can do it!" Ian cheered her on, and Ivan copied his brother as he always did.

Sirens sounded, and a big rig pulled up with flashing lights. The vehicle disgorged a row of firemen who went to work immediately. Jazz made it to the road, and Wolf snatched her from the ladder just as soon as he could reach her.

"What the fuck?" He held her close in a one-armed bear hug since Isaac was in the other one. Jazz felt his whole body shaking. "I'm gonna spank you later for going back into a burning house, but for now, I'm so fucking glad you're alive."

Jazz would have answered him with some sort of smart-ass bratty rebuttal, but she was too busy trying to keep her lungs in her chest. She fell to her knees and tried her best to cough them out. Ian and Ivan sidled next to her on either side as she heaved and spasmed. Her throat burned with the fire.

This is what it must be like on Venus with all the sulfuric clouds and heat. What an absurd thought at this time.

A flurry of activity caught her attention. Several paramedics were working on a strange man who was lying on his back in a pool of blood. She pointed to him, trying hard to ask a question.

Wolf squatted down awkwardly, balancing himself and the baby. "Tugger, your bodyguard for the night. The medics say a car might have hit him."

"Got... call... Liz," she choked out. "How... boys?"

"In a minute, baby. Let them take care of you. The boys are fine. All of them. They didn't breathe that shit nearly as long as you did."

Dizziness hit her, and she rolled to her back. No, that was a fireman who moved her. An oxygen mask came down over her mouth and nose, and cool, clean air filled her starving organs.

"Vitals are good. You're a very lucky lady."

She tried to give him the live-long-and-prosper sign, but she was too tired to move. Her fingers waggled at the hard drive still jammed in her waistband, and Wolf cursed under his breath as he plucked it from her stomach. One of the paramedics took the baby to be examined, and Wolf pulled out his phone. "Ian, what's your mom's number?"

The boy's face was streaked with tears as he stammered out the number. Ivan wailed and lay down on the ground next to his aunt as if he could absorb into her. "Please be okay, Auntie J!"

She shifted her arm around the boy and continued to cough. "I'm gonna be fine, Tribble-butt. Just gotta get some clean air in me."

The oxygen mask helped a lot, and the kids were a great distraction from her own pain. She didn't want to think about what just happened. Her house, furniture, and clothes. All her treasured memorabilia. Her precious books, pictures, and memories. Gone. Just gone.

It hurt.

It hurt as a personal violation.

No way was the fire an accident. Both sides of the house had been alight. The acidic chemical smell had to be some sort of accelerant.

Someone had hurt Tugger and set this up deliberately. The Slaggers were her first thought, but they didn't have anyone capable of finding her via a deep network dive. She had covered her tracks too well for anyone but a hardcore professional to find her.

An icy chill arrowed down her spine. Whoever went after the other shielders had come to town. It was the only possibility that made sense. She needed to talk to Copperpot ASAP.

Once she had her voice back. Her throat felt swollen and heavy.

She heard Wolf yelling in the background.

"Goddammit, woman, get your fucking ass here! Now!"

Must be having trouble getting Liz to cooperate. Jazz wasn't surprised, but it made her angry. Liz and responsibility mixed like oil and water.

She moved to sit up, and Ian did his best to help

her. "It's almost daytime. Where are you gonna live now?"

The innocent question was a good one. She could take the boys to their grandparents' house, but that would probably stir up drama she just didn't want to handle at this time. All of her bank cards were gone. Her computer too. She'd dropped her phone somewhere in the burning tangle of bushes when she crawled across the ladder, so it was probably gone as well. At least she'd kept the hard drive safe. Her eyes still burned and watered from the smoke. "I'll think of something, kiddo. For sure."

Ian sniffed as he sat next to her. "My dad's never around, and Mom says we're a pain in her ass. Gramma complains about us all the time. Grampa just sits around the house." His face screwed up in pain, and he started crying. "Nobody wants us, and your house is all burned up."

An imaginary knife cleaved Jazz's heart in two. "Hey, buddy, I got your back. I really, really do. Pinkie promise and everything. I know your mom loves you, even though she yells a lot and stuff. We'll have an adventure, yeah? We'll go get pancakes at Denny's for breakfast with an ocean of syrup. I'll figure everything else out later, okay?"

She hated this. Her nephew was too young to

have to deal with all the shit life just heaped on him. Not even in school yet and already he had to grow up fast because his parents couldn't be bothered to actually do the job.

Freya! "Where's my cat?" she croaked.

Ivan pointed. "Over there."

Freya had evidently forgiven Wolf for tossing her across the dip. She sat next to him with her leg in the air as she groomed her fur. He brushed the phone's screen with his thumb and addressed the ragtag group.

"Hospital first. Quillon's wife kept her place as an Airbnb rental. Three bedrooms, and it's open. That's where we're going to go once we get everyone checked out."

Ivan popped up from Jazz's side. "Can we still have Denny's pancakes?"

"Sure, kid."

"Is my mom coming too?" a subdued Ian questioned.

Wolf gritted his teeth. "She's not answering her phone. I'll keep trying."

"Can we ride in the amble-ance?"

"Sure. Now hop up, and let's get this show on the road. Everyone needs to get checked out, yeah?" He turned to Jazz as the paramedics lifted Tugger into one of the vehicles. "Camshaft is coming over with his big truck. He'll take Freya and get us set up with supplies for tonight. I'll wait for him and then go to the hospital."

The boys were excited about the sirens and the drive to the hospital. Jazz was worried about the cost and all the chores she had waiting for her. It was overwhelming even for her. The list of tasks grew longer in her brain. Insurance had to be called. The bank for new cards. A computer, as that was a big need for her. Clothes. Diapers. Food and litter box for Freya. A thousand items filled her to-do list during the ride to the hospital. She added even more after they arrived.

Questions about insurance and guardianship came up for the boys. Fortunately, the social worker was satisfied when Ian identified Jazz as his aunt and caregiver. All three boys were physically fine, which took one load off Jazz's mind, but none of them wanted to go anywhere without her. The two oldest hung out in the curtained alcove crowded around the bed, the baby napping in a rolling crib, until Wolf made his appearance.

"How ya doin', babe?" he asked as he leaned over to kiss her forehead.

It was only then that she cried. "My house is

gone. I have to tell my parents and my brother about it. I have to call the insurance people. I don't know where Liz is. I can't... I can't...."

"I'm not going anywhere, babe. We'll get through this. I promise."

"How's Tugger?"

Wolf's grim expression told her all was not good there.

"I'm real sorry about your house, Auntie J." Ian sniffed.

Jazz swallowed her fears and ruffled his hair. "It's just a house. I can get another one. What I can't get is another super-cool nephew like you. I need to introduce you to space, the final frontier."

"Is that the one with Luke Skywalker?"

Jazz's jaw dropped. "Dude, we so need to improve your education. Once we break outta here, it's pancakes, then *Star Trek* classics, pronto."

33

The naked man lay back in the bed and watched the lazy fan turn. It did little to cool the room in this summer heat, and this cheap motel had no other form of air-conditioning. It suited him and his purposes, though, as the place was off the main roads, and the desk clerk made a point of not looking or speaking to him. Every morning he slid cash through the ridiculous chicken wire fencing of the front desk, and the sour-faced person behind the questionable protection took it. That was the total of their interaction, and he was fine with it.

He should have been ready to leave this place.

He should be on his way back to his home in Khyber Pass.

He should be done with this last job he was hired to do.

Instead, he was pissed.

The fire was supposed to take out the final target, but somehow, she escaped her death. It bothered him, as very few times in his life had his plans failed and the victim survived. His tasks were carefully built after observation and research to make them seamless and unnoticeable. Shooting someone on the street in most cities would trigger police investigations and some media coverage. Watching someone drop dead from a heart attack brought on by poisoning his morning coffee, well, that was natural causes with no need for fussy attention. He preferred to operate quietly. Get the job done and get paid.

He sighed and put his hands behind his head. His body was lean and cut, his skin glowing a shiny bronze. Various scars dotted his chest from burns, cuts, and in two cases, bullets. One of those bullets came from his carelessness at a gun testing range in Khyber Pass. The other came from carelessness during one of his first assignments.

The blonde whore he'd fucked to get information said she liked his scars. They made him look tougher than the pussies at the strip club. He smirked. Yes, he was tougher than the pussies at the strip club. He'd seen them there when he scoped out the place to find his target. Old men trying to stay relevant in a world that didn't want them anymore. The Slaggers club was worse. Young men too stupid to recognize their insignificance. He had slight respect for Wolf, but that still didn't amount to much. They were all collateral damage as long as he finished the job and eliminated the target.

He stared at the water-stained ceiling and made his next plan.

34

Jazz threaded her fingers together and flexed them outward from her chest. Several knuckles popped in the silent room. This was so not going to go over well with Wolf, but he was dealing with club shit.

It had to be now.

She took a big breath and shook out her hands. Snacks were laid out next to the keyboard, and two water bottles sat in front of a bank of three borrowed monitors. She'd already peed in preparation. Once she started, she wouldn't be able to stop until the job was done. It would be hours, and taking a break would be impossible.

She glanced into the main living room of the Airbnb.

Hugo snored lightly as he lay back on the sofa. He came to visit her more often now, and she figured he was in protective-brother mode. Isaac was sacked out in the playpen with all four limbs limp against the mattress pad. These were two of the reasons she did this. There were many others. Her other nephews, who were at a church preschool, Bill and Madge, Liz, her parents, and of course, Wolf.

She sniffed back tears as she thought about all they'd been through these last few months.

She had to succeed. There was no choice.

"May the force be with me," she muttered as she closed the door to her makeshift computer room and settled into the shaped gaming chair. She moved the keyboard to a secure position on her lap and leaned back to get comfortable.

The mouse moved easily and swiftly under her palm as she opened the dark net to dive deep into the cyber ocean waters. Her search was for the markers she'd placed the last time she submersed herself in this world.

It was hard to find them. Several false fronts were constructed to seem like the original site she sought out, but her signs were distinct. It took almost an hour to break through to where she wanted to be, digging through the pathways until she came to the center of the information vortex. Codes, numbers, sequences, all running in long columns as this criminal enterprise continued.

What would happen if she shut it all down? Could her special virus do it?

She needed a worm. One that replicated itself and jumped from network to network as a carrier of the virus.

Copperpot created a worm once. He showed it to her before he destroyed it. Scary stuff. Combine it with a virus and it would be an unstoppable disaster. Attack the electrical grid? Screw up missile targets? Bankrupt an economy? The damage that kind of duo could do would be catastrophic, and in the wrong hands, it could destroy entire countries. It was tough enough to keep control of the virus at all times. If it got away from her....

Nope, it couldn't happen. There was no alternative.

The banks these people used were easy to hack. No, not people. They weren't the ones who went to work every day and did their best to provide for their families. These were criminals, and she had to remember that. Parasites that thought nothing of stealing from others' hard labor, taking and taking and taking until there was nothing left.

She delved deeper, searching for that central place where she'd been once before. The dark web was a maze that twisted back on itself, sometimes blinding the explorer with dead ends and circles. Page after page, site after site, she clicked and moved, testing links, trying different codes, backtracking and covering herself as she hunted for that sweet spot she needed.

Then she was there.

It was no less terrifying than the last time she was here. Streaming lines of numbers fell down the screens. Dates, times, transactions, phone data, millions in dollars and other world currencies, exchange rates. The beast was massive and interwoven with legit areas. People in multiple countries, all over the world, were being targeted. She would have to go in as precisely as a surgeon to make this work.

A burn started in her sinuses, a prelude to tears gathering in her eyes. She could either destroy or heal, and it was a crapshoot which way it would go.

She sniffed and wiped off her cheeks. "Let's do this."

The numbers flowed, and she watched for her chance. Just a chink. One little opening. Yes, she could force her way in, but that would leave a direct trail back to her. Whatever happened, she had to keep herself and her people safe. If anyone was really looking for her, that could lead them to her family. Her nephews who had lost so much. Hugo, who was scared to leave the group home campus by himself now but still insisted on being with her after what happened. Her parents, who still housed and took care of Liz. Bill and Madge, two people who just wanted to make a living and enjoy their lives.

And Wolf. The man she once watched and dreamed of from afar, now in her bed and in her life for the long haul.

There it was. A break in the numbers. It was small, but it was all she needed.

Her fingers flew over the keyboard, and she moved to upload her virus.

She hit Send.

Nothing.

The virus file bounced off, deflected as if a glass wall protected the streams.

"Shit!"

Another chink appeared, and she tried again. The code bounced off like a horse swatting away a fly.

"Someone put an iron-coated firewall around this sucker." Jazz's tears dried up as frustration took their place.

Another opening.

Another bounce.

Three times rejected. How long before her repeated attempts got noticed?

Sweat gathered on her brow as she tried a different approach through a back channel. The file shot back so fast, she had to duck in a game of cyber dodgeball.

She made more attempts, and they got thrown back at her with increased force. If she kept this up, she would eventually trigger an alert about her intrusion in the system. They would discover her lurking about, and if she wasn't careful, it was possible to trace back and find her physical location. She rerouted herself again and erased her tracks, but with this sophisticated network, it might not be enough.

"I gotta get this right."

Another try, and another rejection. She growled under her breath. "There has to be a way in. Just one spot."

A break appeared, and she went for it. Again, the upload was deflected.

Jazz slammed her hands down on the desk, and the force zinged up her arms. Tears filled her eyes again, both from pain and frustration. People were being victimized right in front of her eyes, and she was powerless to stop it. The personal violation she felt when the Slaggers destroyed the coffee shop was nothing compared to what she experienced now. The sheer magnitude of what was happening on her computer screens made her want to scream. *Unfair* wasn't a good enough word to describe the level of dishonesty and downright cruelty of these cyber scammers. She had the means to safely stop it, but how the hell to get in?

Jazz dashed the moisture leaking from her eyes and placed her fingers on the keyboard. Her hands shook with emotion, but she had to keep trying.

A sudden ping sounded, and a small pop-up window appeared on her screen. It wasn't part of the scam network but a separate message.

Message: I can help you.

Fear threw her off at the unexpected guest. How did this... whoever it was... find her here? She was supposed to be off the grid and hidden.

Message: I have a way to get in.

She rerouted, but the messenger stayed with her.

> Message: I can make a gate for you.
> Please let me help.

Against her better judgment, she messaged back.

> Anonymous: Who are you?

They answered immediately.

> Message: We've never met, but I
> want the same thing you do. These
> people have to be stopped.

> Anonymous: Why should I trust you?

Jazz held her breath as she waited for a response.

> Message: I can't give you a reason.
> But I have what you need to take
> this network down and keep it down.
> Let me show you.

A link appeared.

> Message: Click to see, but don't
> download or open it.

Jazz hesitated. Clicking on random links could be devastating. It could let loose a virus in her own system. Even though this was a separate hard drive from her work and personal information, anything was possible in the cyber world. Any little footprint she might have missed in her purging and rerouting could spell disaster for her or her people.

> Message: Please. Look at the margins. They know someone is here, and they're looking.

Sure enough, there were searching codes that appeared along the edge of the stream. She was still hidden for now, but it wouldn't be long before they found her. She had to get out now and give up on ever stopping this shit or....

> Message: There's not much time. I'll hold them off as long as I can, but please click the link so you'll see I'm telling you the truth.

A rapid set of numbers appeared, blocking the searchers and sending their quest away from her. At least for now. Jazz wasn't totally ready to trust this person, but the quick and thorough diversion path was impressive. It twisted a bit like a curve in the road. *Elegant* was her first thought.

> Message: I can't hold them off for
> long. They will figure it out and come
> back. Maybe stronger. Maybe more.
> Please check out the link.

Jazz grabbed the top of her head with both hands and let out a long "Grrrr" at the screens. She checked her firewall protections and saw they were secure. She'd built them herself, strong enough to withstand photon torpedoes. This guy… person… whoever was messaging her hadn't tried to batter his way into her computer. He did lead the search codes away from her hiding spot. Was he legit? She felt like the person behind the screen was male, but she didn't have anything to go on other than instinct.

What did her instinct tell her now?

She blew upward into her bangs and removed one hand from her head. Her palm came down over the mouse, and before she could talk herself out of it, she clicked the link.

A smaller window opened up, showing lines of code that were all kinds of fucked up.

A worm. This guy was showing her the inner workings of a worm.

Computer worms were different from viruses. They were made to replicate themselves automatically, jamming up networks and jumping from place to place without anyone's help but its own. This one was a doozy.

> Message: Hook your virus to this program. I'll make a way to insert both into the network.

> Anonymous: How do you know this will work? Who are you?

> Message: I'll explain everything once we take this beast down. The worm is a special program that is designed only to hit and damage certain networks. When it's finished, it will destroy most of itself but keep the original line in a safe place. If the network ever triggers again, it will come out and start over.

Uber-cautious was the keyword of the day, but something about this person made her think he was legit. Gut feelings had helped her in the past, and she'd learned to trust her instincts when it came to certain decisions. But could she do that now? With so much at stake?

> Anonymous: What happens if it gets away to other networks?

> Message: It won't. I made it to only recognize this network. Please, we have to do this now before it's too late.

Jazz's fingers hovered over the keys, itching to make something happen. Anything. The worm's language looked complicated as it writhed on the screen. She wished Copperpot was around to advise her, but according to Stud and Table, he wasn't in good shape.

In the corner of one screen, she spotted the searchers turning and coming back. This time they would find her and trace her.

She said a prayer to whoever might be listening in the universe.

> Anonymous: Okay.

> Message: Follow my lead.

She stared at the screen. Her vision blurred at the numbers darting ceaselessly across the monitors. She recognized she was crying aloud but had no idea what emotion made her do it. Frustration, fear, helplessness, hope, relief someone else was aiding her, or some combination of all the above. She was almost in a state of euphoria when she saw it.

An opening.

Wide and inviting.

A gate.

Message: Do it now!

She didn't need him to instruct her, as she was already typing, her fingers hitting the keys heavier with her efforts. Before she could second-guess herself, she hit Send. Her hands stilled their frantic movements and hovered over the keyboard. She watched as the worm burrowed further into the program, her virus riding on its back. Line by line scrambled and fell away, disappearing somewhere into cyberspace.

"We did it." Tears flowed down her cheeks, and she sobbed openly now, with no one around to stop her from letting it out. She felt all squishy, floaty, and a little out of control as she viewed the permanent destruction of this evil network. The structure was massive, but the worm and virus were unstoppable. It burned through the scammer codes, decimating it into nothing. It was slow but thorough, and Jazz was actually impressed with its ingenuity and finesse.

A message popped up.

> Message: It's done. Check this link
> when you can.

Jazz sniffed and grabbed the closest cloth object she could reach. It turned out to be one of Isaac's burp towels, but at least it was a clean one. She wiped her face on the dancing elephant in a pink tutu and made a mental note to throw it in the laundry basket. Her hands came back to the keyboard.

> Anonymous: Who are you?

The dots stayed still for several minutes, and she was about to give up when they started bouncing.

> Message: I'm called Nassar. Kindly
> check the link. It will expire in ten
> minutes, so do that now.

So, it was a man, and he gave her his name. It might be fake, but Jazz didn't think so. The links looked legit, and so far this guy had been a straight shooter. She clicked the link, and it brought her to a bank account.

"Holy shit!" The expletive left her mouth open. There were so many zeroes, she would have to count them to find out how much money was there.

> Message: I saw you give back once
> to those who lost. Here's a part of
> what's owed. I know you'll do the
> right thing for the right people.

Jazz's tears started again.

> Anonymous: Yes, I will do that. Since
> you told me who are, I feel as though
> I should do the same.

> Message: NO! Do not tell me your
> name or handle. I can't keep you
> safe if I know who you are.

Jazz brought the burp towel to her face again with one hand while she typed.

> Anonymous: Thank you.

There was really nothing more to say. She sat back in the chair and flipped the elephant towel over her shoulder. The worm kept moving farther and farther to the margins as the virus rode out its mission of destruction. When it was over, the worm turned in on itself and disappeared. The code for her virus went with it.

It was truly over.

Well, not yet.

She leaned forward and tapped into the money-stuffed account.

Yes, she knew what to do.

NASSAR LET OUT A LONG-HELD BREATH AS THE last of the criminal network vanished. He rapidly typed to erase the last few messages. The agent in charge had left the room to pee and grab a cup of the swill they called coffee, leaving Nassar just enough time to send a link to Anonymous. The officer had spent hours watching every keystroke Nassar made during this operation, but the past five minutes was just enough to get the message out about the money.

The constant surveillance was nothing more than what he expected. The time he'd spent when they first detained and interrogated him was worth this moment. His plea for asylum was ignored until they decided to take a chance on him. He'd spent days repeating over and over again how he wanted to help and had the means to do so. The drive he'd smuggled from the call center so many months ago turned out to be his ticket to freedom; otherwise, he would still be stuck in the specialized prison, praying and hoping for a miracle.

It came in the form of this anonymous user he stumbled onto while the agents watched him hack through the dark web. He didn't know anything about this person, but something about their mannerisms made him think it was a woman on the other side of the keyboard.

He sensed a trust in her and hoped it wasn't misguided.

The agents were interested in finding her and recruiting her to their cause. That would paint a big target on her back, bigger than the one she already carried. He hoped his actions would erase it and she could live a long, full life.

The agent entered the room and placed a cup of the noxious brew next to Nassar's elbow. "You did well today. I don't know how much of a pardon you'll get, but I can say that the higher-ups will thank you for your work. Might even offer you a job."

Nassar breathed a long sigh. "If I have to go to prison, I'll do that. But I will not do any more of this kind of work. I just want to live a quiet life with my wife and my children."

The agent took a swig of the brown liquid and grimaced. "Guh. Nasty." He put the cup down and pulled at his tie. "Uncle Sam might have other plans. It would be in your best interest to listen to him."

Nassar shook his head. "I will hear the words, but my mind is made up. I can't be a part of this world anymore. I've hurt too many people and should make atonement."

The other man grunted as he sat heavily in the chair next to Nassar. The plain room was soundproof and hack-proof, so anything said or done would be off the grid. "Atonement, eh? Maybe you should think about that. Wouldn't working for us be a way to make things right?"

Nassar paused. "I hadn't thought about it that way. Perhaps I should consider everything before deciding."

The cybercrimes agent gestured to the keyboard. "What about your buddy there? Think they'd want a job?"

Nassar shook his head. "I don't know who that person is, where they live, or anything about them. They're so hidden I cannot find them."

"That good, eh? We really should recruit that kind of talent."

"That would be impossible, sir. There's no way of finding them."

"You sure?"

Nassar inclined his head. "I am very good at what I do. This person is much better."

The agent sighed and shrugged. "It was worth a shot."

Nassar's back relaxed. "There's nothing left to do with this network. It will never come back."

"Others will take their place."

"Yes, they will."

"That's what you'll be doing if you decide to work for us. Taking them down."

Nassar smiled. "I will rethink my position."

35

Jazz panted with effort and picked up her speed as she cruised through the neighborhood on her preferred form of transportation. She was at loose ends. No work at the bakery for now, no work deadlines, and no scam baiting. She was too restless to read books or watch her favorite TV. Her skin itched from the boring confinement. Maybe a visit to Hugo and the dog treat place was in order. At least it would give her something to do and somewhere to be. Wolf was down at the club, meeting with the other members about what the future would held with him as president.

What exactly did that mean for her? Was she now a club queen? She'd watched *Sons of Anarchy*, but that was a TV show and not how real motorcycle clubs worked, right?

Gah, she thought as she pedaled onto the bike lane heading to the bridge. She had other issues more important than what her club status would be.

Liz finally showed up and had a complete shit fit over her kids. She promptly pointed her finger at Jazz while angrily cussing and accusing her sister of negligence. That was totally rich, considering no one could find her for almost twenty-four hours. Still, their mother capitulated, and the boys were back with their grandparents. No one thought to contact Leo.

Jazz felt sorry for her nephews' predicament, but legally, there wasn't much she could do other than be supportive. Her last words to Ian were "Call me if you need me" before Liz took them to dump on their grandmother.

A few cars whizzed by, but she was too lost in her head to pay much attention to them. One car stayed behind her for some distance but then turned off on a side road. Just before she reached the bridge, she noticed the deep rumbling sound of many motorcycle engines. They were behind her and coming up fast.

Shit! She took the exit for the bridge and didn't dare look to see who it was. *Could be some other riding group and not one of the MCs. No one is going to worry about a single bicycle rider. Mind your business and keep moving.*

The plan was a good one, but unfortunately, it didn't work. Jazz found herself surrounded by loud motorcycles as they crowded around her about a third of the way onto the bridge. The signs said no motorcycles in the bike lane, but that didn't stop them. She had to brake hard when two bikers cut her off. The Slaggers logo blazed from their cuts.

"Well, well, well, isn't this a coincidence? Look who's out for an afternoon ride." Ramrod dismounted and swaggered up to Jazz. "You owe me some fucking money, bitch."

Her entire body locked into place, and her heart revved up to the point of explosion. "What?"

"You heard me. I know it was you who fucked with our accounts. You're gonna come with me to the clubhouse and put it all back. You get me?"

Play dumb. I don't know what you're talking about. What money? "Dumb money talking."

He snatched her from the bike, pulling her jacket taut around her throat and lifting her to his sneering face. "Don't fuck with me, cunt. I got a computer guy prospecting with me, and he says you're some sort of cyber genius. Someone took our money, and that someone is you."

One of the other Slaggers picked up her bike and heaved it over the side of the bridge. Jazz counted to ten twice before she heard the splash of it hitting the water below.

"It's your lucky day, bitch. You get to live long enough to get our accounts full." He pulled her cell phone from his pocket and stuffed it into his own. "If you're a good girl, I'll shoot you quick. If you fuck around, every one of my guys is gonna take turns fucking your ass while you choke to death on my cock." He pulled her closer, and she smelled his sour breath. "Then I'll kill your family, starting with your fucking brother."

She couldn't breathe enough to respond. Of all the scenarios she'd planned for, this wasn't one of them. How did they find out about her? She always covered her tracks with the utmost detail. No one should have been able to find her. Not even Copperpot. What happened?

Ramrod let go of her throat, and she fell to the hard ground, gasping and choking. Another biker jerked her up by the arm, and she cried out in pain.

"Shut the fuck up, bitch, or you'll follow your fuckin' bike over the side."

They forced her to mount behind one of the riders and then took off. Jazz held on gingerly, helmetless and scared spitless. All she could think about was Hugo, the boys, her parents…

And Wolf.

Miracle rescues only happened in movies, and happy-ever-after endings were for fairy tales. Ramrod would no more keep his word than Quark, the Ferengi merchant seeking profit on *Deep Space Nine*. She hoped she could figure out how to keep everyone safe while satisfying the Slagger overlord.

They pulled up to an abandoned store in a strip mall with boarded-up windows in the front. Jazz noted it was the same place that housed the club's bogus dry-cleaning operation. The biker she rode with yanked her off his machine with a snarl. "You'd better get it done quick, cunt."

He shoved her into the closed store, and she fell to the floor. She caught herself by her wrists, and pain zinged up to both elbows. *Are they going to beat me up first?*

Ramrod grabbed her by the hair, and she screamed as he dragged her across the floor. "Shut the fuck up and fix it, bitch." He pointed to an ancient dust-covered desktop computer on the counter that was connected by a hard-wired USB cable. Old tech and not secure at all. Maybe she could send out a message to someone. Anyone.

A folding metal chair was slammed in front of the box screen. "What the fuck are you waiting for? Get to it."

With trembling hands, she lifted herself to the chair and turned on the monitor. A voice in the background made a tsking noise. "She's not going to be able to use that thing. It doesn't have the necessary RAM."

"She's gonna get rammed if she doesn't take care of business," one biker guffawed while the others laughed. One of them started playing music out of an old boom box while another pulled out an array of liquor bottles.

Jazz heard a drip of disgust at the man's next reply. "Not ram as in fuck. RAM as in random access memory. This one doesn't have the capacity to do what you want her to do."

There was a light accent to the man's baritone. Jazz stiffly turned to see him. He had on a leather jacket, and she assumed he was part of the club. "Y-y-you're right. I c-c-can't do anything with this machine. It's too old."

His dark eyes met hers, and the blood froze in her

veins. There was nothing there. No emotions. No hate. No love. No anger. No happiness. The man was void of life, yet still walking and talking. She watched as he raised a finger to stroke over a scar near his left ear.

This was him. The one who'd killed her friends, the other scam-shielders.

No, she wouldn't be getting out of this alive. But she would fight until her last breath to keep others safe. "Do you have a laptop or something with at least DDR4 or DDR SDRAM?"

His black eyebrow rose. "Yes, I have an upgraded system."

"Well, bring that shit in here. I want my fuckin' money," Ramrod yelled in frustration.

The man took his attention from Jazz and jerked his head to the back of the store. "It's ready to go."

Jazz stumbled along the short hallway to what might have been an office at one time. The room was small with a row of awning windows close to the ceiling. Two of them were open, and the other two were painted shut. A small skylight let the sunlight shine down on the card table with two large monitors, a keyboard, a mouse, and a powerful desktop. If she had any doubts about the man's identity, there were none now.

"You want a snack and some water?" Ramrod sang out sarcastically. "Get your ass to work!"

Jazz bit her lip to keep it from trembling and sat in the wobbling office chair as she booted the computer up. The machine went through its beeps and clicks as it awoke.

"Hurry the fuck up!" Ramrod shoved her just behind her neck, and she gasped as she snapped forward. Her hands hit the edge of the table so her face wouldn't smash into it.

The assassin made that tsking noise again. "It takes a while for the computer. Patience. You'll get all that's coming to you."

"Whatever," Ramrod growled. "I need to take a piss."

Jazz flared her nostrils to take in a large breath as she pulled herself up. She could not afford to break down the way she wanted to. She licked her lips and tasted blood. Apparently, she'd made contact with the table anyway.

"So, I guess you're the one who... killed my friends?"

"Yes."

The cold answer wasn't menacing. If anything, it sounded bored.

"Why did you do that?" She could see his reflection on one monitor. She focused on it, trying to glean anything she could from him.

"I was hired to do a job. I did it."

"Those people who hired you are criminals. They take advantage of elderly people and steal from others who are just trying to make a living. It's not right."

"Not my problem."

"The shielders were just trying to help those people. What if it was your mother or your sister who was robbed?"

His reptilian eyes met hers on the glassy screen. "I don't have family. I suggest you get to work."

She shuddered and placed her hands on the keyboard. "We were so careful. You must be a real whiz at code in order to find us."

The man's expression didn't change. "Not my job. The man who built the code ran away. We can't track him."

"How did you find me?"

He shrugged. "I don't really know or care. I was told the head programmer who escaped has a tracking program that was modified. It wasn't easy to break through his code, but it led me to CatLady50. Unfortunately, that tool was lost when you destroyed the network."

So, he didn't know coding or computer language or anything like that. There was a chance. It was a long shot, but it was her only option at a happy ending.

She put her hands on the keyboard and started typing.

36

WOLF WAS ALREADY OVER THIS PRESIDENT bullshit. Quillon had pulled up a template for bylaws and standing rules the club needed to adopt and follow. Today's meeting was about wording them to meet their needs. The legalized language was giving him a migraine already.

"It says we need a two-thirds majority quorum in order to enact a vote. What the hell is a quorum?"

"Point of order!"

"We haven't discussed anything yet."

"I know. I just always wanted to say that."

Fuck me! Wolf pulled out his phone and fired off a text.

> Wolf: Yo, Stud. You guys have bylaws and shit like that?

The reply came in seconds.

> Stud: Yeah. What's up?

> Wolf: Can you share them with me? I'm trying to herd cats here and could use some direction.

> Stud: I can't make a unilateral decision for my club, but I'll bring it up to Brick and see if it's possible. I'll let you know.

He closed his phone only to see Melter rolling a blunt. "I don't see what the big deal is. A few sales now and then won't hurt us. We can take over where the hippie guy left off. It's just a little weed."

That was the last straw. Wolf rose from the round table and took a breath to cuss the shit out of the older man when his phone jangled. His blood ran cold as he heard the sound. It was the one he'd put in for Jazzy in trouble.

Just then, someone started banging on the front door.

"It's Denny," Camshaft announced.

"Denny, we're busy right now—

"You need to get un-busy," the officer said as he entered the room. "We got a tip that a girl got taken by the Slaggers on the Fleming Bridge. Someone sent us CCTV footage proof, or at least that's what we think. The video showed up at the office on every computer screen. Hard to tell from the angle, but I'm pretty sure that's your woman."

Wolf's blood froze in his veins. "What the fuck did you just say?"

Denny turned his phone around and showed Wolf a short reel. The image was grainy, but he could clearly see Ramrod with his hand around a woman's throat. A moment later, a bike sailed over the safety rails of the bridge, and she was forced on the back of another man's motorcycle.

"Meeting adjourned. Get the fuck out."

No one questioned his decision. Not even Melter.

Wolf turned to Denny, his voice harder than titanium steel. "Where?"

"We don't know. Got them getting off the bridge and heading north, but the traffic cams are out. We... I was hoping you would know."

Wolf checked the text he'd received on Jazz's ringtone. It wasn't a message but a map link. Somehow, Jazz got ahold of a computer and sent out an SOS. He swallowed the fury building in his throat and chose his words carefully. "That wasn't Jazz on the bridge. Probably some chick Ramrod wants to get to know better."

Denny's eyes narrowed. "Are you sure about that?"

Wolf's gaze dropped to a frosty zero. "Positive."

Denny sighed as if resolved. "All right. We're gonna dig up some information and find the Slaggers' place. Prolly take a few hours. I'll give you as much time as I can, but my help will only go so far. You get caught, you're paying for it."

"Thank you, Officer."

Denny shook his head. "Just do me a big favor and don't do something that will make me arrest you for real, yeah?" He muttered several curses under his breath as he left the club.

Wolf was alone. He didn't roar with unfettered, burning rage. He calmly walked to the back locker room and picked up a hard-sided case he'd stored there. A few minutes later, he was on his bike and heading north.

"WHAT THE FUCK IS TAKING SO GAWDDAMN long?"

Ramrod sucked back a lungful of sweet smoke and blew plumes of it in the air. Jazz coughed at the pungent smell of pot and typed in another random line. "I've pulled out the funds from the orphanage and got them deposited in your account. The other transactions are processing."

She silently prayed her message got through. She'd piggybacked a link into a text when she hacked into her own phone. Then she set up several phony accounts that showed huge amounts of money. Every time she "transferred" from one of them to the Slaggers' account, it showed up as pending approval. That was enough to keep Ramrod happy and smoking as he saw his numbers go up. Jazz had no idea if she was fooling the other guy. He hadn't said much since she started pressing buttons.

"Fucking cunt. So stupid to spread my money all over the place."

"A really big deposit would trigger an automatic audit. I didn't want any of those charities to get in trouble." She didn't know if that was true or not, but it sounded like a legit excuse. The longer she took, the more time she gave Wolf to find her. She had visions of him and the club bursting in and razing the place to the ground. Or maybe Wolf would have an unstoppable John Wick moment. There was also the chance that he hadn't received the text or would get here too late. "My family doesn't know a thing about this. As far as they're concerned, I'm the big fuckup. There's no reason to go after them."

"Stupid bitch." Ramrod took another long drag and held his breath. He spun the shaky chair around and backhanded Jazz across the face. The chair tilted, and she ended up on the floor.

A small quick *chink* accompanied her cry of pain. Ramrod's head snapped back, and a clean red hole appeared in his forehead. The look of surprise on his face stayed there as he crumpled next to Jazz.

"*Madarchod!*" The word burst from the assassin's mouth, and he seized Jazz's hair to yank her up and put her body between his and the window. "You did this, didn't you?"

Jazz's mouth filled with a warm coppery taste. Ramrod's blow had reopened the cut on her lip, and blood was flowing again. "I never touched my phone. Ramrod still has it."

He laughed. "Do you think I'm stupid? *You* don't have to use your phone to call someone. The question is, did you call many or only one?"

His grip tightened in her hair. "I think only one."

He stepped back to hide in the shadows of the small room and placed Jazz in front of him as a shield, pulling her head back and slightly to the side so she was forced to stand tall and arch her back. He rested a large handgun on her shoulder with the barrel pointed at the windows. The angle of the sun shone down on Ramrod's body, still bleeding from the head wound.

Minutes passed. Jazz's head burned from the unrelenting grip, and her shoulders were starting to cramp from being held in the awkward position.

"Call him."

"What?"

"I said call him." He pressed a burner phone into her hand. "I want to hear what he has to say."

The first time she called, it was ignored. It took three times before Wolf picked up.

"Hello."

"Wolf?"

"Tell him I'm going to kill him."

The line went dead. Jazz whimpered at the matter-of-fact tone in Wolf's flat voice. Just like Stefan in *The Vampire Diaries*, his emotions were turned off. The person he hated from his past, he'd gone there again.

"H-h-he said—"

"Yes, I heard him. Funny, as I believe I'll kill him first. Pity, as I feel this man and I are brothers in a way. We now play a game of waiting and stamina. Who will win?"

"You sound amused."

"I am, *priya*. This is the first time in a very long while that I've had a challenge. Most of my assignments are simple and boring. This one has entertained me more than anything else in years."

Jazz's voice was crushed under the need to cry or scream. "I don't suppose you'd consider letting me go? I'm so done with the scam-shielder thing. I just want to protect my family."

He clicked his tongue. "It's nothing personal. Just a job."

"I find this very personal."

The assassin gave a short laugh. "I see what my rival likes so much about you. We have several options. We can wait for him to make a move. From this angle, I can see everything. The movement of the sun, the shadows, anything that comes through those windows. From the trajectory of that bullet, he's not that far away. Probably on one of those higher rooftops a few streets over. It would take him quite a bit of time to break down his weapon and move to a more advantageous location. The problem he has is there is no other alternative but to target us directly through those windows."

Jazz's eyes welled up, but she didn't move to dash away the tears. Through the film of moisture, she looked up and envisioned Wolf spotting them and lifting a gun just before the assassin took him out. Would she be able to stop it? Push the guy or become deadweight he couldn't hold on to?

The man continued to talk as if he was ordering a pizza over the phone. "The second option is to move to the exit. This would require exposure but very little risk to me, as you're a very good shield. The sunlight will enhance your coloring more than mine; therefore, I'll be invisible as you radiate. He won't be able to see me. That is if he's still in position. If he's moved to get closer, he won't have any sort of visual. He will also have to handle more than one man. There are many guns in this place. With so many targets, he would be hard-pressed to kill us all." He chuckled. "It might not even be me who shoots him."

A new emotion rose in Jazz's mind. Anger. "I will never understand why anyone thinks it's okay to rob older people of a lifetime of work. To take advantage of someone who's desperate and lonely. Or cheat someone out of their hard-earned money when they're looking for a break. People who just want to work, pay their bills, and live in peace. It's not right, and it never will be."

"What does that have to do with me killing your boyfriend?"

"You wouldn't be here if those scummy scammers weren't in business."

"You're right, but you'll never stop it. Con men have been around for a long time, *priya*. Centuries. They've just moved into the internet realm, that's all."

She sniffed. "Yeah, well, I changed my mind. When I get out of here, I'm gonna keep being a pain in the ass to them."

This time his laugh was deafening in her ear. "Oh, my precious girl, you're not getting out of here."

Jazz's heart clenched. Both she and Wolf would die today. Someone would find the bodies and wonder how they got there. Hugo would be devastated. Her mother would beat her chest and cry to all the neighbors. Liz would mourn in her own way. The boys... what would happen to them?

"I think we'll use option two. Let's move." He started to shuffle against the wall, keeping her body in front of his and always facing the rectangular windows. The gun stayed resting on her shoulder, the barrel next to her ear. The sun was blinding for a moment as they moved, and Jazz squinted against the bright light. The movement was awkward, and several times she tripped over her own feet, causing her hair to be pulled in the man's tight fist. It felt like her scalp was going to rip from her skull. She had the absurd thought that she hoped someone would get her a pretty blue wig for the funeral.

Who'm I kidding? Mom will donate my body to science. She won't spring for a casket. Maybe crema-tion? "Spring for my body cream."

She didn't realize she'd spoken out loud until the man behind her stopped. "What are you talking about?"

There was no little *chink* this time. One moment she stood next to the office door, her back pressed tightly to the front of the assassin. The next seconds were a blur. The door opened, and Wolf suddenly appeared with no sound or warning. His arm was up. Jazz heard a single *pew*, and the man behind her crumpled. The gun he held over her shoulder fell to the ground. The man didn't have time to react or even see Wolf until the bullet had traveled through his head and out the other side. His dead face sported the same surprised look as Ramrod's.

For a millisecond, Jazz was scared. Scared of Wolf. His eyes were completely devoid of emotion. No color. No life. No love. The gun was still in his hand, pointing at the spot where he'd fired into the assassin's head. Then she saw it. Those green-and-gold orbs changed as if a switch had been flipped. With a single anguished noise, he pulled her into his arms, and she felt his trembling body.

"Fuck, fuck, fuck, fuck!" he chanted. His shaking got worse as he clutched her to him.

She put her arms around him as best she could. This was Wolf. The man she'd loved for years before he really became hers. This was the man who accepted all of her and her crazy family. This was the man who saved her life and the lives of her nephews. This was also the man who gave up a piece of his hard-won humanity to come save her again. "I'm okay, love. I'm okay."

For minutes they stood simply holding each other as close as possible. Wolf finally let her go and lifted the palm of one hand to his wet eyes. "We need to go. Denny is probably on his way by now, and we can't be here."

"What about the other Slaggers?"

"They don't know anything has happened yet. Between the loud music and the drinking, they didn't hear anything. Plus, the suppressor did its job."

"The silencer?"

"We call them suppressors. They reduce the sound a lot, but they don't eliminate it."

"Oh. How did you get in?"

"There's a side entrance that was blocked. I unblocked it."

"Oh."

So simple.

"I'm gonna block it again when we're out. We need to make that now, baby."

"Oh."

"Jazz. I need to know you're with me."

Shock was setting in, and Jazz sensed she was shutting down. "Yeah, I'm with you. I just need to do something real quick."

"What?"

She moved from his arms to the computer, leaning over the keyboard and rapidly typing in a stream of code. "I'm setting up a false front and erasing any traces of me on these transactions. They're all fake, but if anyone digs in, I don't want anything to be left behind that could be traced. Maybe it will seem like they had a fight and shot each other."

"The men in the other room will remember you being here."

She shook her head. "It's their word against mine, and I'm hacking the cameras at Attic and adding footage that shows both of us at the club when all of this happened. I'll purge the bridge video, too, so there's nothing that can tie me to them at all." She tapped the keys, filling the small space with fast rhythmic clicks.

A faint siren grazed the air.

"Are you finished, babe?"

Jazz hit the Enter key. "Yes, let's go."

37

WOLF LISTENED TO JAZZ'S MOAN AS HE SANK deep into her body. She was pressed up to the shower wall in the Airbnb, her arms over his shoulders and her legs wrapped around his waist. Hot water sprayed over them as they moved.

He'd soaped her up and washed her hair, taking care not to cause her any pain from the bruising or the cut on her lip. When he looked at her injuries, he wished he would have taken the time to beat the shit out of Ramrod and Mr. Happy, the moniker he gave to the assassin since he never told anyone his real name.

"I'm done," she announced on a heated breath. "I'm not going to go after any more scammers after all. I won't take another chance on someone I love getting hurt or dying."

He thrust in slowly, savoring every stroke as her channel caressed him. "I didn't plan on ever picking up a gun again, but as far as I'm concerned, this is my last time, too, sweetheart. I just want a clean, easy life with you and the club."

Jazz barked out a laugh and realized she was crying at the same time. "You think the Knights will be at peace?"

"I can dream, right?"

His movements became firmer, and her gasps of pleasure grew more pronounced. His balls tightened, and he was on the verge of coming. "I fucking love you, Jazz. Don't ever change your hair or your words or anything about you. This is real, baby. As real as it gets. You worked your way in with cute and coffee. Now you have to stay with me."

She cried out as she found her release. He joined her half a second later, letting his roar of satisfaction reverberate in the tiled room.

"We didn't use a condom again."

"No, we didn't, and I don't want to. I like feeling you come while I'm inside you." He kissed her lightly as he withdrew and let her legs down to hold her own weight. "If you want birth control for a while, we'd better get on that soon or else I'll have to move up my plans."

"What plans?"

He grinned as he plucked two towels from the nearby rod and handed her one. "I fully intend to put a patch on your back sometime this fall and a ring on your finger by Christmas. You get pregnant before then, I'll move my plans up a few months." He rubbed the white cotton cloth over his head and wrapped it around his waist. "The insurance from the fire is a good start to rebuild the house, and I have some money set aside. I've already told you about a potential design I have in mind. We can go over that sometime this weekend if you're up for it."

He paused as he picked up a comb and turned her around to face away from him. The teeth glided through her wet hair as he smoothed out the blue strands. "How's your head?"

"It doesn't hurt."

"No, baby. I mean, *how's your head?*"

She stayed silent for a moment. The last few days and even months had been a series of trials. A lot of shit happened between the first scam-shielder dying and the kidnapping from the bridge. It wouldn't shock him to find her dealing with some mental acrobatics and justifications. He was prepared to be her counselor or find her one if she needed it. Instead, she leaned back against him, and his arms folded up around her towel-clad torso.

"I'm good. It bothers me that people are dead, but I don't believe that's my fault. If it could have been avoided, that would be better, but if I have to make a choice between Ramrod or my brother, it's going to be my brother. The same with you and Mr. Happy. I'm sorry he's dead, but I'm happier you and I are still alive."

He kissed her temple. "If you ever get weird thoughts or feelings, you'll talk to me, yeah?"

"Absolutely. Will you do the same?"

He paused with his lips against her skin. "That's a big ask from someone like me, baby, but I promise I'll do my best."

"Okay. Hey, don't you have to go to work tonight?"

"Nah. Cam's covering for me at Attic." He leaned back and continued to comb through her hair.

"Oh."

"That 'oh' sounds confused. What's on your mind?"

She tilted her head back. "It's nothing really."

"What's nothing?"

"Just an odd thought. Why do you call the bar Attic? It's on the ground floor of a business row."

Her innocent question had him smiling from ear to ear. "From what I understand, Melter came up with the name. Attic is actually an acronym."

"An acronym? For what?"

He let out a chuckle. "Wanna know the joke? Look at your chest and spell the word."

"Huh?"

He coughed to keep from laughing out loud. "Look at your chest. Now spell *attic*."

Her head bent forward. "A-T-T-I-C." She put her face in her hands and let her wet hair slide against her cheeks. "You've got to be kidding."

He scooped the strands back with the comb. "Nope. Those jagoffs decided Attic was a good name for a titty bar, and that's why."

He let go of his laughter at her groan and kissed her again. "You hungry?"

"Not really. You?"

He pulled the towel from around her breasts and dropped it to the floor. "I'm starving."

EPILOGUE

"I FOUND ANOTHER ONE!" HUGO'S EXCITED CRY came from down the pebbled beach. He held up a shiny green piece of sea glass to show his sister and brother-in-law before adding it to the collection bag at his hip.

"I got one too!" Ian held up his own treasure. Behind him, Ivan sat on the ground and poked through a pile of smooth round stones.

September temperatures sat in the mid-sixties here in Belfast, Maine, so swimming wasn't a good idea in the rocky bay area. Still, Jazz's brother wore his swim trunks along with his hoodie "just in case."

It had been just over a year since the scam-shielder group imploded. So much had happened during the last ten or so months. Liz found herself a generous man who appeared to genuinely care for her and the three boys. Her tongue was as sharp and critical as ever, but it didn't seem to bother Reginald in the slightest. He smiled at her demands and gave her what she wanted most of the time, although he did stand up to her when he needed to. Jazz had seldom seen her sister back down, but Reggie had no problem keeping her in line. As long as the boys continued to thrive and grow, Jazz was cool with her brother-in-law.

Leo was still around, but he didn't call or visit his kids. Jazz was pretty disgusted with him, as he'd signed over his parental rights with no hesitation. When he walked away, Jazz was glad to see him go.

Bill and Madge were ecstatic to find their accounts full again. The email from the bank stated they'd found a glitch in their system and their savings had been drained erroneously. They had corrected the mistake and added the interest that should have been earned. Neither Bill nor Madge questioned the windfall. They didn't reopen the bakery, as Bill's health was never going to get better, and they decided to rest easy for a change.

Wolf was now the official president of the Iron City Knights MC. Scrap still sat in his spot at the strip joint and gruffed at anyone who disturbed his chess game with Baghouse or Melter. Otherwise, all decisions about the club's direction were made by Wolf, Quillon, and Camshaft. Go-Kart would be getting out of prison soon and would rejoin the Knights next spring if all went well.

What path the Knights would ultimately follow remained to be seen.

Jazz waved at Hugo as he found another piece of sea glass, then turned to see what Wolf was doing. On the deck above the beach, she spotted her husband manning the grill with her mother close by "supervising." Her father was also on the deck, minding his own business as usual. Liz was in the hot tub while Reggie stayed indoors with the napping Isaac.

When Wolf had promised a road trip, she didn't think he would include her whole family. The three side-by-side cottages they had for the week belonged to a cousin of his who lived in Bar Harbor. Liz and her group stayed in the bigger one while their parents and Hugo were in another one. The smallest of the three was off a little farther to the side and a bit more secluded, which was what Wolf wanted for the two of them. All three gray-colored buildings were connected with a large community deck and hot tub.

Jazz raised her nose and smelled the grilling steaks on the wind. Dinner would soon be ready. She turned and called out, "Okay, all Vulcans and Romulans, report to the mess hall!"

Hugo grinned and yelled back, "We're not Vulcans and Romulans. You're so weird!"

As the boys scrambled their way over the rocky beach, Jazz's phone dinged. She saw a text from Copperpot. He'd kept his handle even though he'd also stopped baiting scammers online. Both he and Jazz decided it was pointless to keep doing what was essentially trying to behead a hydra. Instead, they spent a lot of hours developing an app that prevented scammers from getting to their targets. Yeah, there were a lot of scam-call blocking apps, but this one was all-inclusive with emails, texts, calls, and any other form of communication. Not only could a subscriber protect his or her devices, but they could add an extension to cover family members who may or may not be able to protect themselves. It was a great way to ensure no one bothered a grandparent with Alzheimer's or a person like Hugo, who might not be able to distinguish scams from legitimate communications. Once the app was launched, the subscriptions poured in like crazy.

Copperpot: App stats are up if you want to take a look later. Everything is running smooth. No hackers can get through our firewalls.

Jazz smiled as her thumbs raced over the screen.

Jazzyhands: Very cool. How's the diet coming?

Copperpot sent back a vomiting GIF.

Copperpot: My prez hates kale with a passion. Now I know why.

"Jazz! We're about to eat!"

Jazzyhands: I gotta go stuff my face with my man's meat. TTFN!

Jazz giggled as she clicked off before Copperpot could respond. She mounted the wood steps that led from the beach to the deck and sidled up to Wolf as he pulled the steaks from the grill.

He tucked her under his arm and kissed the top of her head. "Everything good, baby?"

"Everything is perfect."

The End

ACKNOWLEDGMENTS

I had many inspirations that drove me to write this story. Scammers are a big one in that there was a time when I was completely inundated with scam emails, texts, messages, etc. Bugged me a lot! Then the algorithm gods sent a bunch of YouTube videos to my feed that were about people baiting and hacking scammers, leading them on wild-goose chases and generally wasting their time. I loved it, so I decided to write about it.

I also have to say a colleague of mine inspired me to create Hugo. My friend's daughter, Katie, is a person with Down Syndrome. Katie is a perfect little girl, all smiles, and one of the happiest kids I've ever seen. I wanted to include that joy in this book. Hugo works for a dog treat company, which was inspired by one that is based in Greensboro, NC. Arkbarks specifically has people with disabilities and developmental challenges working for them, baking dog treats. I love their mission to help people post–high school to find a place to thrive. Check them out here: ArcBarks –

DogTreat Company: https://arcbarks.com/

I can't do anything without the team at Hot Tree Publishing. I have the best editor ever in Kristin Scearce. I give her a run for her money every time I submit something. Donna Pemberton, Lori Gries, the great Becky Johnson, and the rest of the crew at HTP are top-notch. We've been working together since I hit Send on my first book. Love all y'all bunches!

My betas, Brittany Shore, Annie Roberts, Mandy Pederick, Andrea Robinson, and Sharron McKenzie, I'm so glad you're on this team, keeping me straight and answering my questions no matter how lame they may sound.

I need to mention my shop partner, David Hohe, in that regard. More than once, I've turned from my workbench to ask him something like "What's the best way to get rid of a body?" and he always has an answer. Little scary, eh?

Lastly, I have to thank the people who read my books. Words will never be enough to say how grateful I am to be writing and having people enjoy the stories I put on paper. Y'all rock!

ML Nystrom

OTHER BOOKS BY ML NYSTROM

DRAGON RUNNERS MC

Mute

Stud

Blue

Table

Brick

Dodge

Weatherman

MACATEER BROTHERS

Run With It

Ready For It

Hold It Close

Risk It All

Give It To Me

THE DUTCHMEN MC

The Price of Redemption

The Price of Forgiveness

The Price of Peace

The Price of Atonement

ABOUT THE AUTHOR

ML Nystrom has had stories in her head since she was a child. All sorts of stories of fantasy, romance, mystery, and anything else that captured her interest. A voracious reader, she's spent many hours devouring books; therefore, she found it only fitting she should write a few herself!

ML has spent most of her life as a performing musician and band instrument repair technician, but that doesn't mean she's pigeonholed into one mold. She's been a university professor, belly dancer, craftsperson, soap maker, singer, rock band artist, jewelry maker, lifeguard, swim coach, and whatever else she felt like exploring. As one of her students said to her once, "Life's too short to ignore the opportunities." She has no intention of ever stopping... so welcome to her story world. She hopes you enjoy it!

Join my newsletter:
www.mlnystrom.com/contact

facebook.com/authorMLNystrom

instagram.com/mlnystrom

bookbub.com/authors/ml-nystrom

ABOUT THE PUBLISHER

www.ingramcontent.com/pod-product-compliance
Lightning Source LLC
Chambersburg PA
CBHW030521190726
48283CB00006B/1715